THE DRAGON'S AFFIRMATION

PERIDOT DRAGON SHIFTER BROTHERS

MARIE JOHNSTON

LE PUBLISHING

Memphis

Introducing humans into our world is dangerous enough, but when my twin's mate has a worried brother who charges in at the wrong time to see me in full dragon mode, it's downright deadly. To save all our scale-covered behinds, I take the brother as my mate. I might've spared him, but I'm the one who has to live with a guy who's bitter about our circumstances and revolted by me.

Vaughn

Memphis is the most sinful-looking woman I've ever met. But that's the problem. She's not a woman. I've seen what she can do, and it's terrifying. I'm a doctor. Violence and chaos turn me off—until I get a glimpse of the toll being a ruler of a small town full of dragon shifters takes on her. Yet if I start seeing her as a partner, a real person, I have to accept that I gave up everything to keep my sister safe. My practice. My home. My lonely single life. I'm little more than a prisoner, but the more I'm around Memphis, the harder it is to care.

CHAPTER

ONE

emphis

WAS THIS MY CURSE? I'd overstepped my bounds and had to suffer? The sexiest male—a man in this case—was forced to mate me to keep his life, and he hated me. My penance was getting growled at every day—ignored at best.

I dressed in my favorite torn jeans and black T-shirt. Going down the hall and through the living room of my home showed me the same view I'd seen since I'd moved in. Nothing and no one. Vaughn Kelso had commandeered my home office. He was up to work before dawn and stayed behind the closed door well after I'd gone to bed. He ate and slept in the office like it was a tiny apartment within the house.

I would be more offended, but I wasn't the one forced to mate.

Technically, I had also been forced to mate. I could've killed him and moved on, the typical process for dealing with humans who learned about our kind but weren't part of our clans. Mating was the only way for a human to become a part of a dragon shifter clan. Death or mating, either would've protected my people. If I had killed an innocent, albeit prickish human, there would've been a few rocky years. Vaughn was the brother of my twin's mate. Maverick wouldn't have quit talking to me. A long silent treatment, maybe, but he knows our laws almost as well as me. His mate Cricket would've hated me, and no one would've blamed her.

Something had needed to be done with Vaughn. He'd seen me in all my dragon glory, killing a treasonous member of my city council. Then he'd seen me shift back to my human form and stand over the headless body. Normally, the accidental sighting would have my head on a block, but I was the ruler, and Vaughn had driven unnoticed into the middle of town. No one had thought to stop an unfamiliar visitor during a termination.

We were a little at fault, but Vaughn and I had paid the price.

Being a doctor, he didn't take to killing. He'd also been forced to give up his lucrative position as a pediatric physician in a hospital in Las Vegas to move to northern Minnesota and work as an online practitioner, stuck in that office twenty-four seven.

So yeah, he was hating life and me.

In the kitchen, I made my favorite breakfast sandwich. I was a sucker for a McDonald's breakfast burrito, but it wasn't often I could leave Peridot Falls and enjoy a fast-food meal. It wasn't often I could leave Peridot Falls. The only reason I had left was to find company for the night—hard to get laid when I was born and raised in this tiny town. The options had already been sampled, and there was a reason I was closing in on my midthirties and still single. Vaughn might not want to touch me, but I'd honor our bond and quit going to the cities for sex.

My stomach rumbled as I assembled three burritos for myself and another three for Vaughn. I didn't know what he liked, but it seemed like a dick move to only cook for myself when my life hadn't been disrupted that much. It didn't matter that the plate often sat untouched in the fridge. Or that once I'd found the pancakes I'd made in the trash when I got home from work.

Take the high road, Memphis, my mother had often said. She'd ingrained into me the duties of my position. The expectations. The daunting tasks looming over my head. I had enough violence in my life, I didn't need to invite more in by lobbing breakfast burritos at an infuriatingly closed office door.

I finished wrapping the last burrito when the office door squeaked open. Didn't he realize I hadn't left yet? Maybe he was sneaking to the bathroom. He probably thought I couldn't hear, but I had shifter hearing and he didn't. That squeak when he snuck across the hall to the bathroom was the only way I could tell he was home half the time unless he was talking to a patient or in a meeting.

Footsteps drew closer. He didn't realize I was still home.

He turned into the kitchen and jumped. "Christ. I thought you were gone."

Hurt ricocheted through me. It was one thing to suspect he avoided me but another to have confirmation.

A part of my brain could've continued to lie to me. *He was only getting used to the change. He didn't hate me. I'm a treat!*

I hated how hurt combined with arousal. Good thing he couldn't sense my attraction. The way his gray slacks hung off his frame—could pants be commanding?—were hard enough not to ogle, but his white dress shirt was hanging open like he had a call earlier and couldn't wait to strip it off, or he was getting ready for an online appointment and would button it right before the camera turned on. Either way, his abs were on full display. His coppery-brown hair was expertly tousled—styled, or did he just wake up?

Maybe he did a ton of pushups and sit-ups in the office. I didn't hear him grunting. He was the quietest human I'd ever met. But his pecs and rippled stomach were hard and a flash of me licking down the plane of his stomach popped into my head. I'd never get that image out. Did I want to?

"Nope." I gestured to the wrapped items on the plate. "Made you some burritos."

The permanent scowl his sister swore was his norm strayed to the food. Reddish-gold whiskers with a touch of gray covered his cheeks. My fingers itched to run over them.

"You don't need to do that." Oh yes, his voice really was that deep.

"I'm making them anyway." I shrugged and took a bite of one of the burritos.

His gaze tracked the burrito to my lips and ripped away. "Are you trying to block my arteries to get rid of me?" Disdain dripped from his words.

I flopped my food on a paper towel and added the other two I'd made for myself. "You know me," I said sarcastically before I cocked my head. "Oh, wait. You don't."

I took my food and slammed out the garage door to keep from having to pass him to get out the front door. I bypassed my obnoxiously red Dodge Ram in favor of walking. Peridot Falls was small enough I didn't need to drive. My brothers lived farther out than me. Maverick was on the outskirts and Levi had a nice place in the country, but as the ruler of Peridot clan, I felt like I had to be more accessible.

My chest was tight for the whole walk, and I'd lost my appetite. I shouldn't expect Vaughn to like me. We were in this together, but he didn't see us as a team.

Maverick was lingering outside the city hall building when I arrived. His hair was closer cropped than our brother Levi's. Levi wore his longer and often pulled it back to secure it. Maverick had a corporate look. All of our hair was dark brown, almost black. We looked alike, but I was the one who dressed like I didn't care. I found my style more useful than the slacks and polo shirts my brothers seemed to favor.

"You're early," I said.

His gaze landed on the burritos and interest grew in his eyes. "You gonna eat those?"

He knew if I hadn't eaten them by now, I wasn't going to. I shoved the bag toward him and took the satisfaction I could at seeing someone devour my food.

"Is this what Vaughn gets to wake up to?" Maverick asked around a mouthful as he followed me inside.

His question was a cold pail of water splashing over my head. "I don't know what he wakes up to or goes to sleep to. Honestly, I don't know what he eats. He does his best to avoid talking to me."

I went into my office. Maverick didn't follow. He stopped in the doorway and stared at me.

I wasn't one for pity, so I booted up my computer and went to the little coffee maker he'd gotten for our birthday a couple of years ago. "Want a cup?"

"Memphis."

I ignored him and pushed the pod into the coffee maker.

"Fuck. Memphis." He stepped in and shut the door behind him. "It's been three months."

I'd felt every day of it. "Yep."

"Three months and you two don't even talk?"

His incredulity didn't make me feel better. "Nope. He doesn't like me, and I don't expect him to. I don't need him." The lie rang empty between us.

Maverick gave me a look that said I was full of shit and we both knew it. I lifted a shoulder. There wasn't much to say.

He sat on the chair across from my desk. His office was down the hall, but we usually talked a couple of mornings each week—about our lives, although mine hadn't changed much since our parents died and I took over as ruler, and about the town—how to grow, ways to bring in money, and what issues were brewing or needed to be dealt with. I might be the ruler, but we were a team.

Lately, our youngest brother, Levi, met with us once a week. He wanted to be more involved, and it was nice to hand off more decisions and discussions.

"He's being an asshole." Maverick didn't have to ask it as a question.

"Do you blame him?"

"You saved his life."

I tired of this monthly conversation. "And he saved

my standing with your mate." In my twin's opinion, that would mean as much as saving the life of Cricket's brother. "Does he talk with Cricket?"

From what Maverick had said, Vaughn had practically raised Cricket, and they were quite close. He'd been a helicopter sibling, even as an adult. But since he'd moved to Peridot Falls, he'd been isolated.

"Not really," he said. "I told her to go talk to him, make him get out of the house, but he's hiding behind work. I didn't think he was worse with you."

"I bet he hid behind work in Vegas."

Maverick nodded. "He was all up in Cricket's business, and I'm sure it was so he didn't have to evaluate his lonely workaholic ways."

Well, if that wasn't like looking into the mirror. Peridot Falls was nothing like Las Vegas. I had little more to do than work. Sometimes, I took night flights over the woods. Watched some movies. It wasn't like I could do everything humanly and inhumanly possible like in Vegas. Being a workaholic was a necessity but also justified.

"Get her to be all up in his business now." I should leave well enough alone with Vaughn. The guilt was making me interfere. There was no hope for us. None. The sooner I accepted we were nothing but roommates, the less it would hurt when he rejected anything I had to offer, like this morning.

～

VAUGHN

. . .

I SLUMPED IN MY CHAIR. My back would have a lot to say if I kept sitting this way. I was so damn tired of taking online clients. Since we couldn't meet in person, all I could do was maintenance and refer them to a specialist if needed. While it was refreshing to work with kids who were mostly healthy rather than toeing death's door, it wasn't close to the career I'd had. There were no young residents full of ambition and ideals to mentor. No fellows whose egos were too big for their scrubs. And few staff members to help me get the full picture of a patient. The ones I had were online too.

My adrenaline-pumping career where I'd worked twenty-four-hour shifts in the hospital before collapsing at home just to take calls as soon as I woke up had turned mega boring.

It didn't help that I refused to leave the office if *she* was home.

I tilted my head back and closed my eyes. Flashing bright-green eyes, full of attitude but softer when she was at home—when I wasn't pissing her off.

Memphis Peridot was unlike anyone I'd ever dated. Tall. Straightforward. The women I'd dated in the past— girlfriends would be a strong term—had been at least six inches shorter than me and slender. They might've worked out, but none had looked like they could bench-press me. Yet my type suddenly seemed more like a side cut and glossy black hair that was longer on top, add in the way she filled out a simple T-shirt and those worn jeans that molded around her ass? A butt I could really envision—

Blood rushed to my dick, reminding me that I hadn't so much as jacked off for months.

My wife was a killer.

Wife was the wrong word. We were mates. And I was stuck in this shitty rural town in the middle of nowhere. The edges of a big city were only two hours away, but I hated to leave my sister in order to get some semblance of a normal life.

The faint thuds of a knock on the front door reached my office.

Leaving the room, it was like I could stand straight for the first time in hours. I was sick of this space. Sick of sleeping on the floor, tossing and turning, like I could smell Memphis's vanilla bean scent as if she was leaning over me the whole night. Who smelled like vanilla? I had to get up early and rush to the bathroom, or she'd see me sporting a giant erection. I wasn't leaving jizz tracks in her shower either.

I had nothing else, but I had pride.

At the door, I found Cricket glowing like I'd never seen her do in Vegas. She was happy here. Crazy about Maverick and happier than I'd ever seen her. But just in case, I didn't want to be far away.

"What's up?" I asked. "Did a cow get out—or wait—they probably breathed fire on it and ate it for lunch."

The wattage of her smile dimmed. I was being a jackass; I knew it. I'd always tried to hide it from her, but she knew the real me. I had put on a show for sick kids and their parents all day. At night, I didn't want to act. Now I didn't need to.

"I wanted to see if you could join me for a coffee," she said.

"Oh, sure. Come on in."

Cricket didn't budge. "No, join me at the bakery."

"The one your mate's brother runs?"

"Our mates' brother."

Right. My mate. We were with twins. A cozy convenience if I hadn't been forced. "No, I should probably—"

"Vaughn, get your shoes and leave this house. You're getting anemic sitting inside all day."

"That's not how anemia works."

She cocked a brow. Cricket never used to boss me around. This was a new version of her, one that had probably been around for years but her shitty ex had suppressed. Had I been a culprit in taming her true spirit?

I didn't want to look too closely at that.

"Fine. Let me get my shoes." I refused to wear sweats while on camera. I wouldn't work with a patient in less than slacks and a dress shirt. Scrubs had never been my thing when I didn't have to wear them, and I refused to change because my circumstances were out of my control.

A suit jacket seemed absurd for a coffee shop trip with my sister in a town with fewer people than the hospital I had worked in. I tossed on a knit sweater over my shirt.

I glanced out the window. "Are we walking?"

Cricket's car was parked by the curb, but the bakery was mere blocks away. Everything in this place was mere blocks away. The neighborhood was quiet, but they all were in Peridot Falls. I had a ton of questions about what the dragon shifters in town did—I didn't hear roars at night—but I was too pissy to ask. I didn't want to be here anyway.

"Might as well. It's nice out." She peered into the house. "Huh. Everyone talks about this place like it's a mystery, but it's just a house."

It was my prison. I stepped outside and locked the door behind me. Memphis kept the place locked up, and being from a large city, I did the same.

Fall was approaching, and the slight breeze had a bite. Truthfully, it felt good. I'd been cooped up for months, and the fresh air was long past due. Already, the temperature was as chilly as most Las Vegas winters get. I hadn't experienced a full Minnesotan winter, and I hated the thrill that rose inside me at the thought. I used to love my annual skiing trips. They were what had gotten me through the long weeks.

Cricket rubbed her hands together. She had a thin wraparound coat on. From one pocket, she withdrew a light pair of gloves. "It's getting so cold already, but Maverick said it's a really nice October."

October. Kids would come to my clinic dressed in Halloween costumes, or I'd hear about their plans. The peds floor would party as much as possible to help the kids feel like they weren't missing out on yet another special day. That sort of energy didn't transfer over the screen the same way.

One day I'd quit feeling sorry for myself. Today was not that day.

"You'll have to try one of Briony's scones," Cricket said. "She makes the best orange cranberry scones you've ever tasted."

"I'm not a big scone eater, Bug."

She made an exaggerated show of looking me up and down. "I'm sorry. I'm trying to see how long of a stick you've become to be so stuck in the mud."

I barked out a laugh, unused to the sound coming from myself. "Point taken."

"So," she said so quietly I could barely hear, but that would be because we lived with creatures who could hear way better than us. "How are things really?"

Since we wouldn't be able to talk in a business owned

and run by relatives of our mates, I answered. "Fucking boring. I think I hate my job, and I'm not a fan of being forced into a relationship."

"I know Memphis has a strong personality, but is she really that bad?"

The flash of hurt I'd caught in her eyes before she'd extinguished it with that defiant attitude Cricket was talking about sat heavily on my chest. "I don't talk to her much."

"But you're living together."

The words were sour coming out of my mouth. "I don't leave the office much."

Cricket stopped in the middle of the sidewalk. We were still in the residential area. The next block had the bakery. Small houses like Memphis's surrounded us.

I couldn't avoid my sister's stunned stare. "In three months, you've hardly left the office?"

She wouldn't like the rest of the truth. "Only when she's home."

"Vaughn."

"Bug." The use of her nickname didn't soften her. "We're two people who were forced to be together for some otherworldly rules."

"They're not otherworldly. They're from this world."

"Not from where I'm standing." Memphis and everyone else in this town possessed innate abilities the patients I treated would die for—abilities they could live for.

"They're like us."

When she said that, I shook my head. "Abso-fucking-lutely not. We do not turn into dragons and decapitate others."

Cricket stopped again. "Are you ever going to get over that?"

I was ready to scowl at her and think of a sarcastic response, but her serious expression stopped me. "I don't know. How can you?"

"Knowing the damage that female had done to my mate and her own family? I can move on."

When did Cricket become bloodthirsty? "It's not something I can wipe from my mind. I've dedicated my life to saving others, and now I'm irrevocably connected to a person who destroys them for a living."

"It's hard on her too," she said quietly.

I didn't want to think about that. "She still does it. Murder."

"It's an execution, and she doesn't get the privilege of a judge, jury, and executioner. It's all on her. You put yourself on this pedestal, Vaughn. You like to claim you dedicated your life to saving others, and I do think that's the foundation, but do you think maybe you're using a god complex as a shield from developing feelings?"

"What the hell, Bug?"

She lifted a shoulder. "You think highly of what you do, and you should, but you're not stepping out of the lab coat to give a thought to what Memphis has to live with to do her job and protect her people. She's also protecting humans. What if a shifter decides they don't like hiding or feeling like an inferior being and targets humans? It's Memphis and other rulers who stand between them and us."

"It's a society built on violence."

"Aren't they all?"

I sighed and kept walking. She didn't get it. She didn't

fight death and lose too many times to think on the bright side. Memphis was a monster.

A monster with a tight ass, high tits, and a challenging expression that made me want to see what it took to make her soften, to drop those full lips open in ecstasy. Would she dominate in bed? Or submit? She was a monster who made really good breakfast burritos, and when she took a bite, all I could think of was shoving my cock in her mouth instead of the doughy wrap.

I groaned, and Cricket shot a worried look my way. I forced the memory of the death in the middle of the street to the center of my mind. A bloody head apart from a body. Clear as a bell. But the longer I lived with Memphis, the less impact the thought had on me.

I couldn't let that happen. I was not impervious to violence.

We finally reached the bakery. Construction had started next to the brick building. A future office for the rental places Maverick and Cricket were setting up. More apartments because, apparently, people actually wanted to live in an isolated place like this with nothing but a café, a bakery, the city hall building, and houses. There were other businesses and folks who worked a trade and had home offices. Cricket had talked about plans to open office space in the place going up next door, including a cabin rental business she and Maverick were going to run.

I hated that I was interested.

Inside the bakery, sweet doughy smells filled the air, steeped in the aroma of rich coffee. Memphis's youngest brother, Levi, lingered behind the woman—female, as Cricket would chide me—gathering an order in a large white box. His mate's giggles filled the air, and his low chuckle did not inspire any jealousy in me. At all.

"Levi, we have customers." Briony looked over her shoulder. Both of them knew we'd entered and it hadn't stopped their PDA. Briony could shift into a mountain lion. A baker who could grow claws. Unreal. Delight crossed her face when her gaze landed on Cricket, and surprise when she saw me. "Cricket. Vaughn. What can I get you?"

Levi stepped back. His flirtatiousness vanished, and he watched me with an appraising quality that prompted the competitive bastard in me to rise up. "Nice to see you, Cricket. Vaughn."

"Levi." I would be civil. I squared my shoulders and tried a softer tone for Briony. "Coffee, black." I didn't have time for fancy shit.

Cricket flipped her hair over her shoulders. She was irritated with me. "Get him a mocha-choca-latte. He needs to live a little. And one of your orange cranberry scones for each of us, please."

"Sure thing. Have a seat." Briony's pleasantness and welcoming nature toward my sister weren't lost on me. If Cricket had to move here and live with a guy I'd never otherwise want her with, then I was grateful for...a person who turned into a cat. Damn.

I chose a seat that looked out the window but put my back to the couple who couldn't keep their hands off each other. Cricket draped her jacket over the back of her chair and sat across from me. She smoothed her hands over her thick shirt. For a girl born and raised in Las Vegas, she sure took to dressing like she was in a Hallmark Christmas movie. Her leggings were as thick as the only jacket I had needed in Vegas, and her boots reached her knees.

"How's work?" she asked.

Cognizant that even if we whispered, Levi and Briony would probably hear us, I tempered my answer. "Fine, but I'd rather hear about the home renovations you and Maverick are doing."

Cricket inspected my expression for a moment, like she wasn't sure I was serious. I was. Anything was better than talking about my life, and when Cricket chatted about what she and her mate were doing with their house, she was animated and so damn happy I couldn't help but feel like I didn't epically fuck up raising her. That even though she'd married a guy who could also rip heads off, our parents would be satisfied with the job I'd done after they were killed.

As she was digging out her phone, my gaze strayed out the window like a magnet pulled my eyes in a specific direction at the exact moment Memphis jogged down the steps of the city hall building. I'd been there once, and I didn't care to go again. It smelled like her. Sweet fucking vanilla bean.

I wasn't the one with heightened eyesight, but I was riveted by the bounce of her boobs and mourned when she hit even ground. Maverick was next to her, and he must've said something funny. She smiled.

Goddammit, she smiled. Her eyes lit under the sun as she slapped her brother's chest, and for a few moments, the weight of the community was lifted off her shoulders. She seemed younger. Less severe. Still just as sexy, but a smiling Memphis was approachable. A laughing Memphis was normal. She was dangerous, only I wasn't thinking about death and destruction.

What if I was the one who made her smile?

I shook my head and ripped my gaze away. Briony slid a large white mug in front of me.

"Thanks," I muttered.

Cricket was staring at me, phone in her hand.

"What?" It came out almost a snarl. I'd been busted staring at Memphis.

"Nothing."

Nothing was right. I took a long drink and burned my damn tongue. I deserved it.

TWO

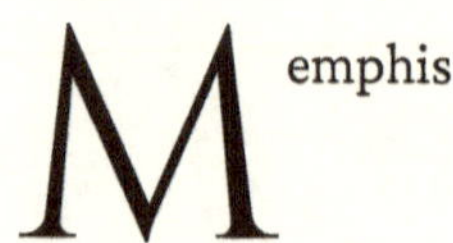

Memphis

MAVERICK CROSSED the street with me. We'd had lunch at the café and were going back to work. I glanced over and caught sight of Vaughn leaving the café. Maverick had mentioned Cricket was going to attempt to coax him out of the house. It'd worked. His dark gaze lifted to meet mine, held for a heartbeat, then slid away.

"Shit," Maverick murmured.

"He's a cold man." In a hot body. Seeing the guy in slacks and dress shirts turned me into a cat shifter. I wanted to purr. Add in the moody way he stalked across the sidewalk next to his much shorter sister, and I was a goner.

"I can't tell what he's thinking," Maverick murmured. "It's odd."

"Isn't it obvious? His expression says he hates us all, especially me."

"What about me?"

"You irritate him, but I think it's only because you're fucking his sister."

Maverick's wolfish grin couldn't be more proud. "We make a lot of sweet love too."

I pretended to gag while stuffing down a sharp rise of jealousy. I couldn't be happier for my brothers, but sometimes their constant state of pure mated joy got to me. Left an empty ache in my chest.

Once we reached my office, Baxter was there. He was the newest member of the city council, replacing Tina, the female I had shredded. The memory still gutted me. I was so angry at that female, but I also missed her. She had needed to be dealt with, but she'd been like a member of the family. Her granddaughter and Maverick had first gotten together when we were teens. Tina had been an envious, conniving pseudo-family member, but still. Family was complicated, and I had never thought I'd have to terminate her.

Now I couldn't sit in on a council meeting without wondering if one of them was next. Were they hiding something? Was I going to be facing them in the middle of the street, planning how to decapitate them as quickly and easily as possible? Would my mate witness it all again and think I was more evil and disgusting than before?

"Memphis?" Baxter broke into my thoughts. He was a guy in his early sixties. I never thought he was interested in clan leadership, but he'd been so appalled at what had happened, like the rest of our people, he'd stepped up. I hoped that meant he was a good guy and not trying to get his own bloodline in the ruling family like Tina had been trying to do.

Maverick's gaze was on me. If he sensed my dreary thoughts, he knew better than to mention them in front of anyone.

"Yeah, Baxter. What's up?"

Baxter's mouth set for a moment. A warning. He had to talk to me about something he didn't want to discuss, or didn't want to discuss with me. I gave my brother a look he could interpret. "Talk to you later, Maverick."

"I'll be in my office." He returned the look. "But I'll check in before I leave."

"Yep." He'd noticed Baxter's hesitance too, and knew the male's news was likely to sucker punch me. "Come on in."

Baxter entered and shut the door behind him. Damn. He sat on the edge of the chair Maverick usually sat in. I took my seat behind my desk and let out a quiet breath. "Whatever it is, just rip the bandage off."

Relief crossed his face. "It's about young."

Fuck me. "Whose?"

"Yours. And that human's." My groan was almost too strong to contain, but I did it. I'd been prepared for my position as ruler but not discussing my sex life.

And that human Baxter was referring to would have to look at me for more than five seconds in order for me to have a kid. That wasn't happening anytime soon. "And just who wants to know?" I almost declared it was no one's business, but that was the thing about being the ruler. It was the clan's business. If I didn't reproduce, then the council would have to make way for Maverick and Cricket's future kids to rule the clan. We'd have to prepare the people so there was no acrimony or other drama.

I'd have to explain why I wasn't having kids. If it was a case of couldn't, that would be hard enough. Telling everyone my mate couldn't stand to touch me would be humiliating.

"The other members of the council were going to bring it up at the next meeting but decided it should be a private conversation."

"Let me get this straight—you all talked about a mix of my sex life and fertility behind my back, decided not to approach me and be straightforward about it, and instead thought to send the new guy to broach the topic, thinking I wouldn't be as offended?"

A flush crept up his cheeks until I wondered if his wrinkles would turn white. "Yes, that's the sum of it."

"I've been mated for three months. What's the rush?" If I was closer to thirty-five, the deal breaker age for getting mated, then I could see their concern. "I've got a guy. Do you all expect me to pop out babies like Nerf darts?"

He licked his lips, the bitter tinge of his nerves staining the air. "You're not— They, um... Some might wonder how maternal you are."

"I don't have to be maternal, just fertile." My throat grew thick. Being told I didn't seem like the motherly type was insulting. I was way beyond offended. A hurt similar to what I felt this morning when I talked to Vaughn hit me. I was the ruler this clan needed, and they questioned *that*?

"Yes, well. It's a concern. The council thought you should know."

"Noted."

Baxter adjusted his glasses like he was waiting for me to say more. I had a lot I could verbally spew, but I wouldn't give the council the satisfaction. I'd had to terminate one of them and this felt a lot like punishment. A stark reminder that I wasn't solely in charge, and they weren't disposable.

"Is that all, or are you all worried about how well I'll please my mate, or maybe if my tits can properly nurse? Anyone want to suggest that I don't shake babies in case I didn't know?"

A deeper red wicked up his neck and into his hairline. "Ah, no. I believe that was all." He got up, straightened his sport coat, and strode out the door.

Since my office was still open, I didn't sag against the desk. *Fuck*. That was humiliating.

I sensed Maverick before he walked in. The soft click of the door was the only noise. He didn't speak.

I stared at the top of my desk, tracing the wood grains. "You heard all that, huh?"

"Yep. The council has balls."

"They're upset about Tina."

"They should be angry at themselves since she did what she did under their noses."

I shook my head and sprawled in my chair. "I mated well before thirty-five. The rest is none of their fucking business."

Again, he didn't respond. He knew better, and so did I. As the ruler, my life was a lot of their business.

"They suspect things aren't going well with Vaughn."

"Things are going nowhere, and apparently, it's obvious," I said as quietly as possible. No one else needed to know how dismal my homelife was. I couldn't take it. It'd been a trying few months, and I needed more time to adjust. My time was up.

He blew out a breath. "Want me to talk to him?"

"Don't you dare."

Maverick's gaze was steady. "Someone should tell him what you're up against. What you both are up against."

"Leave it alone, Maverick."

He held my gaze. A war waged in his eyes. Was he going to drop it?

Finally, he tapped his fingertips against the desktop and left. Instead of burying my head in my hands, I flipped on my screen. Long workdays were my norm since I mated, but just in case Maverick talked to Vaughn, I'd work even longer tonight.

~

Vaughn

I GLOWERED at my dark screen. I didn't know how long I'd been staring, but I'd logged out of my last session hours ago. Night had fallen, and it was late.

Where the hell was she?

I got up and roamed to the kitchen. Opening the fridge even though I wasn't hungry, my gaze fell on the breakfast burritos she'd made me this morning. I slammed the door shut.

Dammit. I'd thrown her food away before, trying to make a point. My own little petty rebellions. A spot of control for a man whose life spiraled into something that didn't resemble his ordered days from before. I'd felt like shit each time. Horrible guilt gnawed at my stomach for days. Somehow, putting the plate in the fridge didn't make me feel much better.

The house was as dark as it was outside. Memphis didn't like a lot of neon lights. The oven time didn't show. Neither did the microwave. There was one old-fashioned clock on the wall, otherwise it was like she didn't want to be hounded by time or duties while she was home.

Every time I walked out of my office, a wave of relief rolled over me. Disconcerting at first and then...pleasant. I couldn't see the clock without turning on a light, so I had to look at my phone. After midnight.

Where was she?

The talk from earlier ran through my head. I hadn't done much speaking, but Maverick had laid out what he'd needed to. Memphis was getting pressured to have a baby. Her maternal instinct was being questioned.

That had to suck. I didn't know her, and she didn't look like the type to coo over a baby, but what that councilman said bugged the crap out of me.

Perhaps because that was supposed to be my baby she was having.

My baby.

A primal need hounded me. I was out the door and halfway to the city hall building before I realized I was searching for Memphis. Minutes later, with the aid of only a few streetlights, I stared at the structure in front of me. One light was on.

In the distance, dark shadows swooped over the trees. Dragons who'd shifted and were flying in the cover of the night.

Would I get used to that?

Since I hadn't noticed until now, I already was.

Sighing, I climbed the steps and navigated the dark hallways until I stood outside Memphis's open door. Her head rested on her arms and her breathing was even.

I took a step forward.

She popped her head up. "Maverick, I didn't—" She blinked and frowned. "Vaughn?"

For a few blissful moments, her guard had been down. The hardness of her expression softened and her bright-green eyes weren't wary. Silky black hair hung over her forehead instead of being brushed back or to the side. She was always sexy, one hundred percent of the time, but now she was approachable like when I'd seen her earlier. Had she tightened up because of my presence? I didn't realize how she wasn't relaxed at her house, but then, neither was I.

She scrubbed her hands over her face and clicked a few buttons on her keyboard. Her edge returned with each passing second. "Is everything all right?"

"Maverick stopped by."

Her shoulders went rigid, and she was back to her usual. "I wish he hadn't."

"You wouldn't have told me?"

Her eyes widened. "Would I have knocked on your terminally closed office door to tell you that we have to procreate? You're a doctor. I'm sure you know you have to get close to do that, and you can't stand me, soooo...not sure how telling you would've helped."

I would have to get really close to that long, lithe body. "I'm aware of how babies are made. I wasn't aware how quickly we had to reproduce." My traitorous mind was filling in images.

"Guess we're in the same boat there." Bitterness dripped from her tone.

"Why are they questioning what kind of mom you'll be?"

She held her arms out like it should be clear, but all I could see were big boobs and a body that would rob me of all thought if she didn't have clothing on. "Guess I don't look like your typical mommy."

"No, you don't." I said it more grimly than I meant to, and her expression reflected that. Like this morning, I thought I spied hurt deep in her gaze. "I've seen all kinds of mothers, Memphis. Appearance and style don't mean a thing, but people get hung up on their stereotypes. I'm guessing shifters aren't much different."

"No. They're not."

I let out a breath as fatigue overwhelmed me. I was tired of the office. Sick of being stuck inside all day. Bored with my job. I was restless, and there was nowhere to direct the energy without running into this female who filled me with too much conflict. Everything about her should be revolting to a guy like me. Nothing about her repulsed me.

"So, we fuck, hope you get pregnant quickly, and they're happy?"

She blanched at my words. "Yeah. I guess."

"Doesn't that bother you?"

"I'd rather be touched by a guy who didn't hate me."

An unfamiliar anger raged inside me. I couldn't put my finger on what was different than the anger I'd carried around since I'd had to move to Peridot Falls. It was me. I was furious at myself. "I don't hate you."

She cocked a brow.

I hated her, partly for how she made me feel. I stuffed my fingers through my hair. "Goddammit, Memphis, this isn't easy for me."

"It's a breeze for me."

That flippant, sarcastic mouth… "I can tell. Working in your office until late, avoiding me when you know your brother might tell me we have to have sex? So damn simple, right?"

"What are we going to do, Vaughn?" The exasperation in her voice was unmistakable. "Get a dozen roses? Some champagne? Book a couple's spa weekend?"

We hadn't even dated. I could take her here. Bend her over the desk. She'd probably comply, and that'd be it. Empty fucking. I'd be fulfilling the rest of my expectations. My dick could quit complaining.

But it didn't seem right, and we both had a full day tomorrow. "Look, it's late. Neither of us wants to do it like mechanical bunnies. Let's just go back to the house and get some rest."

"They're not going to let it go."

"Then I can give them a thorough presentation of how fertility works and prove that if you're really like humans in that regard, waiting a little longer won't hurt."

The corner of her mouth twitched. "I want that presentation, and I want to sit through every minute of it while they squirm in their seats."

Her humor peeked through, and I liked what I saw. A little passive-aggressive stunt that would make all involved uncomfortable. I used to thrive on that shit as a resident—a peon who got pushed around by world-weary doctors and nurses who'd been working longer than I was old. A guy could only be so humble before he had to do some schooling in return. Like dressing as a clown to meet with patients after I overheard a nurse telling an aide a gaggle of clowns could treat the kids better than that year's batch of residents.

But Memphis wasn't a nurse. She was my mate. She was supposed to be the mother of my children. And she was a murderer. She was the reason I was stuck in Bumfuck, Minnesota.

I hung on to my earlier thought. There was nothing we had to do tonight. "The burritos you made this morning are in the fridge. Go ahead and have them if you haven't eaten."

"Sure."

It was the resignation that wormed its way past my righteousness. Murderers shouldn't have hurt feelings. I left before I could acknowledge how much conviction I lacked.

CHAPTER

THREE

My phone blared through a dream where I watched a sinful Vaughn in slacks and a dress shirt saunter into my office with a naughty look in his eye and—

More ringing. Groaning, I popped an eye open. I'd returned from the office before to get some rest in a real bed, but surely it couldn't be time to get up. What time was it?

After ten, with a gasp, I sat up. It'd been ages since I was late for work. Maverick was probably giving me a wide berth since he'd talked to Vaughn after I told him not to. Grabbing the phone, I answered without seeing who it was.

Maverick's voice floated through the line. "The Smalls on the edge of town said they had some livestock go missing last night."

"What livestock? They don't ranch."

"They've been building a hobby farm. Briony was just dealing with them about getting milk and eggs for the bakery."

"A feral?" Feral shifters meant death. Not the way I ever wanted to wake up.

"That's what I'm afraid of. I'll go with."

"No—watch the town in case it's a feral and has lost its entire mind."

"Maybe Levi—"

"Maverick. I'll be fine." My brothers had my back, but I wanted to be left alone today. The talk with Vaughn in my office last night wasn't exactly progress, but it'd almost been nice. I was cranky and sarcastic and he didn't get himself in a huff like a lot of people did when I opened my mouth.

In the hallway, Vaughn's office door was closed. His voice, with a cheerful tone, emanated out, and a high-pitched voice replied, followed by a giggle. Vaughn's returning laugh was hearty, deep, and strong.

He really did like working with kids.

My belly fluttered, and I pressed a hand on my stomach. *Don't go looking for fairy tales in a prison*, and that was what this house was to Vaughn.

In the kitchen, I stopped at the fridge. Inside, the food I'd made yesterday sat on a plate.

Okay.

Any appetite I had vanished. I toed into my boots and walked out. I hopped in my pickup and headed to the highway. The Smalls' property bordered Garnet River territory, but I couldn't risk turning into my dragon in broad daylight.

I pulled into the Smalls' yard after a long meandering drive through thick trees. There were a couple of lakes around the property that were on private land, but that didn't stop shifters of all sorts from making wider trails than the normal game ones that crisscrossed through the woods.

When I got out, I faced a small farmhouse that was well kept with clapboard shutters. The most run-down part of the place was the green-felt-covered concrete stairs that would survive the end of the world.

Bev Small walked out of the front door and down the stairs. "Thanks for coming so quickly, Memphis."

It was my job. I just hoped it didn't end in the worst part of my job. "No problem. Lost some cattle recently?"

Her nod was grim. "With only twenty head, it's easy to notice."

Bev and her husband Darnell grew cattle and chickens, butchered and processed the animals themselves, and sold the meat. They'd built a good reputation and could probably expand if they wanted, but they seemed happy serving the Peridot Falls area and some of Garnet River.

Bev brushed her hands on her jeans. "I left the remains in place, thinking you'd want to look."

We walked across the lawn toward the small pasture on one edge of their property. The fenced-off portion didn't have much for trees and there was a shallow stock pond in the middle. At one time, this area had been used for a camping and recreation area by humans, but when the Smalls bought the land years ago, it became part of Peridot Falls. One of the few ways shifters could expand our territory.

"What's your impression?" I asked as we bent to crawl under a wire fence.

"The carcass was ripped apart like it was for sport."

Shit. A coyote might've gotten lucky with a frail cow, but it'd have chewed the animal from the end up. If the guts were missing, maybe we could blame wild animals. But a slaughtered cow for the sake of killing? That was unstable shifter territory.

Once we stood among the flies buzzing in and out of the remains, I sighed. Bev's description had been apt. The only question was, what kind of shifter was the killer?

"Want to see the other one?" she asked. "It's more of the same."

"No, this confirms enough for me. Have you seen anyone around that's out of place?"

She shook her head. "The only problem we've ever had was when Cecily wanted to date a wolf shifter who worked in Itasca all summer."

A teen daughter and a strange wolf shifter. Didn't bode well. "What's his name?"

"Damon. You don't think it could be him? Cecily's seventeen, and I didn't want her hanging out alone with some twenty-three-year-old who was vague about what pack he was from."

Was he being vague about a pack, or had he been kicked out?

Either way, if the wolf shifter's mental status was trending toward feral, then he was no longer his old pack's issue. He was creating problems on dragon shifter land. If dragon shifters didn't deal with him, he could hurt humans and risk their exposure. "How did he and Cecily meet?"

"He was out hiking and she went to the lake to swim as her dragon one night."

"Not many other shifters like to roam this close to Peridot Falls or Garnet River."

"Right? That's what didn't sit well with me. He gave off a different vibe, but I didn't know him, and it didn't matter. He wasn't dating my daughter."

"What about Cecily? Was she really upset?"

Bev frowned. "For about five minutes, then she met Vernon's son from Garnet River."

"I appreciate the heads-up. I'll look around all day, and if I don't find signs of whoever's doing this, I'll fly around tonight."

"Thanks, Memphis. And if it is something...I'm sorry."

Yeah. I'd be sorry too. If Vaughn had softened toward me, coming home with more blood on my hands would harden him back up.

NIGHT HAD FALLEN. I walked through the house. Vaughn's office door was still closed. There was no talking, but I heard him moving around. Was he getting ready for bed? Working out? The space wasn't that big, but obviously, he was making do.

I'd searched the Smalls' property and followed as many trails as I could until dinnertime. Unfortunately, I hadn't had to wait that long. I caught the smell of wolf shifter. One shifter with a sour tint to its smell, enough to tell me that a feral state was likely. A lone wolf who had been in the area long enough to develop a good hiding place but was deteriorating too quickly to cover all his tracks.

I'd stopped home for a bite to eat. Now it was time to head back out.

When I stepped outside, the town was dark. Peridot Falls used minimal street lighting at night to protect our dragons as much as possible. I stripped on the front step and left my clothing in a pile. Usually, I'd undress inside since I often showered when I returned, but that would be the time Vaughn walked out. Not that I'd care, but he was human and unused to naked beings wandering the town.

He might be used to naked women. I wouldn't know.

After my shirt and pants were neatly folded, I walked down the street. No one else was out, and it gave me a few moments to clear my mind. I'd been alone most of the day, but the concentration had taken its toll. I needed to pretend for a few moments this was a leisurely walk.

At the end of the block, I turned right and crossed the last hundred yards to the trees. As always, I looked around. The one time a human wandered into town, I'd had to mate him to protect him.

Shifting, I embraced the change. A delicious stretch spread through my limbs, nearing the point of pain in my bones, then I was in my final form. Smells were sharper. I could see creatures my heightened human vision couldn't even pick up—mice scurrying through the underbrush and the tail of a disappearing fox. Sounds were easier to hear—jackrabbits in their burrows and birds rustling around their nests.

I launched into the sky and spread my wings to soar over the treetops. The leisurely walk part of the night was done. Now I was working. On the hunt.

As much as I wished the cow killer turned out to be a rabid dog or something, I knew better. The claw marks had been bigger and deeper. Wild wolves didn't take down animals like that. The size fit a bear, but again, bears didn't kill cattle, and thanks to our shifter population, they didn't venture this far.

I flew over the Smalls' farm. Their cattle didn't flinch, used to their owners roaming as their dragons.

I pulled around just as a startled moo cut through the night. Searching for the sound, I swooped lower, skimming the top of the barn and flying farther out. Cows ran to the side of the pasture closest to the house and barn. I went the opposite direction.

Taking in a long inhale, I sorted through the scents. Manure. Chickens. Cats and dogs. Deer. Shifter. Locking on to the smell, I tucked my wings into my sides. A dark form was disappearing into the trees, a loping gait that wasn't the run of a healthy shifter.

Feral shifters broke my damn heart, but I didn't have time to dwell on it.

I made myself as small as possible to barrel down the path through the trees. Branches scraped my scales and my talons touched the ground as I ducked and bobbed. The wolf was running, and a metallic tang tickled my nose. He'd hurt himself.

Just when I was almost on him, he flipped and snapped at my neck. I pulled up short, a heavy tree limb stabbing into my wing.

I hissed, but on my exhale, I blew fire.

The wolf wasn't prepared. He'd likely dealt with regular shifters. Not dragons from a ruling family who could breathe fire.

He let out a yelp and tried to spin to his feet. But he'd already signed his death warrant months ago, and his pack had done nothing, leaving the problem for a dragon shifter to solve.

I didn't chance more fire. Embers smoldered around me. It'd been a wet fall, but I couldn't chance a fire breaking out. I was out here to protect my people, not ruin their property. The feral was staggering, unable to maintain balance after being sprayed with fire. With my talons, I impaled him. His cries tore at my eardrums, but I kept going with teeth and talons until he was limp. Then the final act—removing his head.

Blocking out the sickening sounds, I finished. My sides were heaving when I faced the dead shifter. His body changed from fur and paws to a young human male. A guy who should've been at a bonfire or settling down with a family, but instead, he had succumbed to the high aggression most shifters had to stabilize.

I closed my eyes to catch my breath. The exertion was nothing, which almost made this worse.

Shaking my head, I gathered him to me, heedless of the gore. He needed to be buried. It wouldn't do to have someone stumble onto his remains. My luck, it'd be a human. But I also did it because the act eased my conscience. A life was gone because of me. His actions had brought him to this point. No one would blame me, yet it didn't diminish the toll it took on me to take a life.

Pushing the sorrow to the back of my mind, I launched through the tree canopy overhead. My wing throbbed and my load made my flying pattern wonky, but I made it to one of the lakes. There I set him down and clawed through the soil between two scrawny trees. The burial site would be far enough away from the water's edge and concealed enough to be left alone. The shifter taint to the grave would keep wild animals away.

I'd dug and dug until I had a hole a few feet deep. Fatigue hung on my shoulders. It'd been an active day, but that wasn't why I was tired. First, it was Tina, the death Vaughn had witnessed. Then my mating. And now this.

Dragons didn't cry, but I might in the tub after I'd cleaned the violence off. I always waited until I was alone to cry.

CHAPTER
FOUR

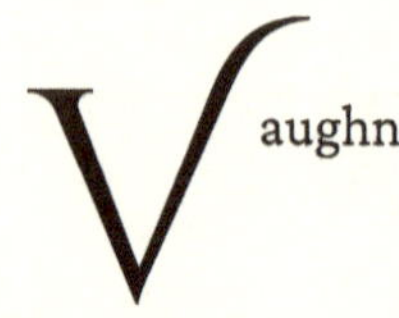aughn

I HEARD the slight movements of Memphis's return. Where the hell had she been? I stared at the dark ceiling in my office. I'd heard her leave. When I peeked outside and saw her undressing, I ducked so fast I nearly clocked myself on the edge of the desk.

She'd whipped her shirt off, and while her back had been to me, it'd been a stunning sight. Muscles across her shoulders. The image of her naked and bloodied from when I first saw her was still stamped in my mind. The longer time that had passed since then, the less horrific those images became and the more I wished I'd paid more attention to how high and firm her breasts were. The flare of her hips and that damn juncture in between that was giving me an erection even now.

She must've gone for a dragon shifter's equivalent of a walk. A fly? I didn't fucking know.

Water kicked on in the bathroom.

Frowning, I switched my gaze to the closed door. Awfully late for a shower.

I listened to the spray until it changed to the heavy stream of a bath being filled.

What the hell did she need a bath for? How dirty had she gotten?

Who'd gotten her dirty?

Irritated, I couldn't sleep, so I got up and crept out the door. Looking across the hall at the bathroom door, I paused. The water was turned down to a trickle.

I padded softly to the kitchen, hoping the light splash of water covered any noise, and drank the half a glass of water I'd left from earlier. Then I stared out the window over the sink. Nothing but darkness. The exact opposite of what I'd grown up with. After a couple of months, I'd finally started getting used to it. It was still weird to look outside after a certain time and see not a damn thing. Cricket said it took her a while to get used to the lack of light pollution too, and now she loved it. Of course she did. She was stupid in love with Maverick and everything was sunshine and rainbows.

A sound caught my attention. I kept my steps light and went back to the end of the hallway. Her bedroom was at the end. She was still in the bathroom. An old place like this didn't have a bedroom suite, just simple square rooms and a separate bathroom.

Another noise, like someone was trying not to be heard crying.

No. It couldn't be.

Someone like Memphis didn't cry. She was too tough.

But in her office, she'd looked so damn tired.

Going even slower because her hearing was so much better than mine, I snuck toward the bathroom.

What was I doing? Snooping? What if she was with another guy tonight and was sad about coming back to me?

Irrational anger swept through me like a dry brush fire.

I stopped outside the bathroom door. Her senses might be better, but she was just as shit at hiding her crying as anyone else. Short, heavy breaths followed by sniffles could be heard.

I didn't question myself. I tried the door handle, and it rattled. Locked. "Memphis."

Another sniffle. "What?" Her voice was thick, like she had a sinus infection. Or like she'd been crying.

"What's wrong?"

"Nothing."

"You haven't lied to me since I've been here, don't start now."

Silence, then a frustrated growl. "Fine, nothing that's your business."

"But you're crying."

"Am not."

"Fuck's sake, Memphis."

"All right, you asked for it." Her voice wavered. "I had to kill a feral wolf shifter tonight, okay? He was killing the Smalls' cattle and it was only a matter of time before he targeted children or humans."

What fucking world did I stumble into? "You killed someone again?"

"Just leave." The anguish in her voice was my breaking point.

The part of my brain, of my personality that saved lives, wanted to argue during my trek to the office. I retrieved the simple tool that would fit into the lock and pop it open. I'd always thought it was humorous. A creature who could tear another apart kept a tool to unlock a door instead of yanking it off its hinges.

Back at the door, I broke in.

Memphis popped her head up from where she was huddled in the middle of the water. The shower wand was on the floor. She'd used the showerhead and then ran herself a bath. Her arms were curled around her knees and her face was red and blotchy, more apparent thanks to her wet hair slicked back off her face.

"What happened?" I asked.

Grief rippled through her expression. She tried to hold strong, her sides heaving as she controlled her breathing. "What I said." Another huff as she struggled to hold herself together. "He was so young."

And she crumpled, burying her head in her arms. Her sobs caused the water to lap around her. I was in blue flannel sweats, but I had boxer briefs on underneath. I yanked my shirt off and stepped out of my bottoms, leaving my underwear on.

I climbed in behind her. She craned to look over her shoulder, her tear-streaked face incredulous. "What are you doing?"

"I don't know. You just seem like you need someone right now, and I'm the only one around."

Her ripe bottom lip stuck out in a pout. "I'll be fine. I'll let myself cry it out and move on."

"Jesus, how many people have you killed?"

She tensed like she was going to get up.

"Sorry, shit." I put my hands on her shoulders and

stretched my legs out on either side of her. The water was a few inches from the top, any sudden movements and it'd slosh over the side. I shut the water off all the way. "It's hard for me to wrap my head around. Do you have to do this often?"

"Too much."

Once would be too much. "Did you know him?"

"No." Her shoulders shook again, and I pulled her toward me.

She cried. I didn't track for how long. There was no clock in the bathroom. How had I thought this female was a cold killing machine? Had she been this upset after I came to town? Had she cried by herself in the bathroom after I called her a monster?

Guilt clawed at my ribs.

When her crying subsided, she lay against my chest. Little sniffles were all that could be heard. The water was starting to cool off, but I couldn't bring myself to move. She felt too good in my arms. She felt right.

"Seven," she said softly.

"Seven what?"

"The first was six months after my parents died. An old bear shifter that was too healthy to die and too lost to keep going. He came up from the city because he knew there were two dragon shifter clans here. Brighton, the ruler of Garnet clan, was too young to do a damn thing, so I took care of him."

"Like suicide by cop?"

She nodded, her hair sliding against my skin. I stroked her shoulder.

"Then there was a mountain lion shifter couple who were just criminals. They weren't feral, but they were using their shifter traits to steal from and then kill families. Maverick helped me hunt them down. Another was part of our clan. One refused to mate. Made it to forty-two."

"You said you had to mate before thirty-five. Is that what happens? You go feral?"

"All shifters are at risk, but dragons are bigger. More aggressive. The feelings get too hard to control and we need an anchor. A bond. The mating stabilizes us. But it's not like we want to kill people when they turn thirty-five and are still single. As much as I wish I could support those who either want to stay single or find someone they'd like to spend their life with, we need that balance. We have too much strength and our restraint weakens over time. We can push the age. As much as we can, but failure to mate is a death sentence."

This was why mating me had solved a problem for her. Mating issue. Done. One of her brothers wouldn't have to terminate her.

I was almost forty. "If I was a shifter, I'd have already gone batshit crazy."

Her giggle caught me off guard. She stiffened like it'd surprised her too. I kept up the lazy circles with my fingers, but she didn't relax.

"One of the people was human."

Her announcement made me freeze. "Why?"

"Levi was out one night and another shifter was getting harassed by this guy. She left with her now mate and the guy followed Levi since he'd been hanging with them. Levi wasn't thinking, and he shifted in the middle of nowhere, but he wasn't paying attention and the man saw."

"So you had to kill him?"

"To protect our secret, yes." The weight of the world was in her voice.

Shit. I should know it was a possibility. That was why I was here. But to hear that she'd killed because of it already...my blood ran colder than the water we were sitting in.

"He was a woman-hating stalker, and he tried to blackmail Levi, so I dunno. It helps when they're horrible people, but mostly it's tragic. Really fucking preventable."

Her bitterness was understandable. A lot of responsibility fell on her shoulders. I came from a profession that did everything to save someone. Death was sometimes inevitable, but it was an outcome I continually fought against.

Memphis had fewer tools and less time, but I sensed she wished to avoid death as much as possible.

"Why you? I get you have to deal with dragon shifters and even the human." How weird was that to admit? "Why do you have to...kill the other shifters?"

"Dragons police all shifter kind." She adjusted her position, and I concentrated on the tile work so I didn't poke her in the side with an erection. The topic was just heavy enough to keep my blood in my brain while I held a naked woman. Female. "We're the apex of everything; the responsibility falls on us. Humans can't know it, or a lot of us would get hurt or studied. We'd never be free. There'd be a lot of death and it wouldn't quit until shifters were wiped out. We might be at the top of the food chain, but humans have sheer numbers on...everything."

"That's a lot to put on you."

"I have Maverick and now Levi. Though we tried to

protect him from it a lot, ultimately, I carry out the termination if I can."

She protected her siblings. She was the oldest, and she protected all her people.

Who watched out for her?

MEMPHIS

I WOKE up next to an oven. Frowning, I blinked my eyes open. The sleep-softened features of Vaughn were what my gaze landed on first. My mind took a few moments to catch up, but I contented myself with soaking in his stubble-roughened chin. The line of his lips, for once not in a downward tilt. This was the first time I witnessed his hair disheveled. Golden and copper tints gleamed in the sun streaming through the windows.

The sun was up? Was I late again?

"Hey." I tapped his shoulder and held in a groan. Squeezing my hand into a fist so I didn't rub over that warm skin covering hard muscles, I tried to wake him again with a light punch to the arm. "Vaughn."

He frowned. Was that the first expression he defaulted to in the mornings?

"Vaughn. It's after eight. Do you have to work?"

His eyelids opened and that hazel gaze of his pierced me. The frown softened, but heat infused his eyes and his gaze traveled over me, stopping at the top of the blankets.

Crap. I was naked, and a breast was poking out. I went to draw the covers up, but he snaked his hand out and lightly touched the tip of my nipple.

That little bit of contact spurred a groan. It'd been a long time since I'd gotten off and a morning Vaughn who looked at me like he could devour me was intoxicating.

He flattened his hand on my breast and massaged my flesh with his strong fingers.

I could succumb. So easily. I didn't know what had altered between us, but yesterday, Vaughn wouldn't have done this. A bathtub breakdown must've done the trick.

"Vaughn."

He rolled infinitely closer. "Yeah?"

Was he going to touch my nipple...with his mouth? God, yes. But, no. "It's after eight."

"After eight for what?" His gaze was hazy and zeroed in on my tits. His movement had pulled the blankets down farther.

"Work. Don't you have to work?"

His eyes flickered, then widened. "Fuck." The loss of his touch was an instant chill as he rolled out of bed. He stuffed his hands through his hair and looked the floor over.

"You left your boxers hanging over the edge of the hamper to dry." After, he'd put a towel around me and tucked me into bed. I couldn't believe he'd crawled in next to me. Otherwise, he had no clothes in my room.

"Shit." He rushed out of the bedroom.

I was alone with a distinct feeling of loss when he popped his head back in. The ruffled hair was sexy as sin, but my gaze caught on his very stiff erection.

"This isn't over between us." He was gone again.

This isn't over between us.

I stared at the wall. What did that mean?

Shaking my head, I crawled out of bed and dressed. His office door was closed and his calm, professional voice drifted through the door. A smile touched my lips and I tried not to hope that he meant he wasn't done with what he started in bed. A steady thrum beat between my legs.

I rolled some breakfast burritos in the kitchen, pausing to drop my head back and take a few deep breaths. It'd be so easy to go into the bathroom and get myself off, but he'd heard me trying to cry quietly. What if I let a moan slip?

No, I couldn't risk it.

My nipples tingled, wanting more of his touch. The rest of my body was jealous.

Shaking my head, I made my breakfast burritos. My hand hovered over another wrap. Should I make him some too? He hadn't thrown away the last ones, but he also hadn't eaten them. If he shunned my food again, it'd bother me even more.

Be the bigger person. I made a couple extra and left them on a plate in the fridge. I munched on my food as I walked to work. The late morning was crisp, like a promise of a new beginning after an awful night.

Polishing off the last of my breakfast, I swiped my hands on my pants. Probably a little more unladylike than the women Vaughn was used to, but then none of them shifted into dragons and killed feral shifters.

Maverick was waiting outside of the city hall building like he'd been watching out his window for me. "What was last night about?"

News traveled fast. "A feral wolf shifter was killing the Smalls' cattle."

"His pack has been calling all morning."

I slowed to a stop. "If it's the guy Bev thought it was, he left his pack."

Maverick shrugged. "The person calling is his mom. Says he was out here working, and he never called last night, but that the Smalls' daughter was toxic and they're worried about him."

I went inside and he followed. "His scent was off. He was feral."

"Maybe he was able to hide it from his family? Or maybe they deluded themselves."

"Or maybe they think it's an opportunity to start some shit."

"There's that too."

When we entered my office, he shut the door behind us. I took a seat and ignored the blinking red light on my office phone. I hated that thing. People could message, but shifters could be old-fashioned and since the city council members were often older, they felt better if I had a loud, blaring phone instead of one where I could turn the sound off.

Maverick sat and propped his feet on the desk. He wore jeans and athletic shoes, going for the less formal look since he'd been getting to work late because he was likely plowing his mate. "How do you want to handle it—since, you know, you don't fucking call me when you're out on a termination?"

"You had someone waiting for you at home."

"When I was alone twiddling my thumbs, you never called either."

It was a sticking point with him, but I couldn't share the shittiest part of my job with someone I cared about. I couldn't put that stress on my twin, no matter how much he insisted.

Vaughn had seen the emotional fallout I hid from my brothers.

I tapped my fingers on the desktop. "I'll call the pack leader, tell her what happened, then see where it goes."

"We'll find out soon enough if it's the pack with the problem or the family." He scrubbed his face. "I don't like either one."

I shook my head. "Me neither."

He leveled an even stare at me. "Does Vaughn know what you had to do last night?"

"Actually, yeah. He, uh, caught me taking a bath."

My brother couldn't read my mind, but he knew I wasn't telling him everything. "And he had a problem with it?"

"Yes." I wasn't happy about what I had to do; I didn't expect anyone to be either. "But I think he understands it's not easy for me."

"It shouldn't have taken him this long."

"You have to admit that seeing me behead Tina was a shock not many humans could just get over."

"Cricket saw, and she isn't shunning me."

"Cricket was already lovesick—and she's not as uptight as her brother."

He snorted. "True. The guy must shit diamonds." He reclined in his chair, hooking his hands in front of his belly. "Did he...treat you all right?"

I fought the heat wicking up my face, but Maverick's bright gaze sharpened.

He abruptly sat forward. "No...seriously?"

"It wasn't like that. I had...a moment...and he was understanding. He was cool."

"Cool."

"Cool." I defiantly held his gaze. I wasn't saying more.

He leaned back. "Interesting."

"I hate it when you get like that. Doesn't Levi need your help with the rental project?"

"One, he's helping me. And two, I won't keep bugging you. I can see you walling yourself off as we speak."

I scowled. Having a twin was as awesome as it was frustrating. "Oh, really?" I scratched my forehead with my middle finger.

He snickered like a good brother and pushed out of his chair. "I'm meeting Cricket for lunch. Want me to bring you something back?"

I'd just eaten, but last night had taken a toll. "Yeah, whatever looks good."

When he was gone, I stared at my dark screen. I didn't start my computer or listen to the messages. Memories of last night played through my head. The most tragic and then the utterly confusing yet comforting.

I sighed and punched the blinking button. Back to work.

~

VAUGHN

I PUSHED AWAY from the desk after my last patient. My boss wanted to schedule a face-to-face meeting in the city. A day ago, I would've been there as soon as he mentioned it. Now I was considering how it'd affect Memphis. How long would what happened last night affect her?

If she bounced back right away, would I hold it against her?

Trudging to the fridge, I stretched my aching back. I needed a better office chair or a standing desk.

There was a knock, and I veered toward the front door. Who would it be? Memphis never had visitors.

Faint sounds of crying could be heard from the other side. Frowning, I opened the door without checking. There were a lot of dangers in town that I was unfamiliar with, but I'd recognize a crying kid anywhere.

A woman around my age stood on the other side. A boy, I guessed to be five or six years old, cradled one of his arms against his chest.

I immediately crouched and put myself on the kid's level. "What's going on?"

The mom backed up a step like she wanted me to have a clear view. "He broke his arm, and I know we heal, but he's been sobbing for hours. Every time he moves, it's like he goes back to the beginning. I heard...you're a doctor?"

"I am."

"Can you do something? He should've healed by now."

Kids liked to move around. He was likely reinjuring the break. My mind spun. I was used to having every supply at my disposal. I called on my first aid skills from before I went to medical school. "What's your name?"

The boy stopped sniffling long enough to say, "Josh."

"Okay, Josh. Let me get some supplies together." I straightened and met the mother's worried gaze. "I'm Dr. V. I'll get Josh's arm immobilized, so it has a chance to mend."

Her gaze was pinched, and she ran a hand through her frizzy dark hair. "I'm sorry to bother you. He's just so active, and I know he has endless energy, but if he keeps using it up to mend the same break, I'm worried..." She pressed her lips together and her eyes darted around.

Was she nervous to talk to me?

"He's in so much pain."

I needed to get moving. "It's no problem. Let me go into the garage and see what I have. You can sit on the steps so he doesn't have to jostle it."

I rushed through the house and into the garage. There I found twine and old pieces of wood. I debated sawing the axe handle into two pieces, but that'd take too long. Josh's arm was too small for any of the wood, but I could use the twine. Inside, I couldn't find any newspapers or magazines. Damn. I needed something with some length and rigid—

Ripping open a kitchen drawer, I grabbed a couple of serving spoons. In another drawer, I found some dish towels. Once I was outside, I jogged down the stairs. Josh was on the bottom step, and I kneeled in front of him.

"Okay, Josh, I've got two spoons, some towels, and twine. Think we can build a fort?" His dubious look was enough to tell me that he didn't think so and he didn't find me funny. "Can I splint your arm, Josh? So it can't move until you heal?"

He shook his head. "No." When he wrenched himself to the side, he shifted the break again. His little body shook with tears.

"Joshy." His mother rubbed his back. "Why won't you let Dr. V. look at you?"

Josh whimpered and she sighed. "Is it your friends?" she asked. To me, she said, "He broke his arm at school yesterday, but his friends said he must not be a real shifter since he hasn't healed."

Ah, kids. I dropped my voice. "What about if we go

inside? You wear the splint until you feel better, then you can take it off before you leave the house?"

"That sounds like a fine idea," the mom said.

Josh blinked at her, pale.

"I'm a doctor. I'm not allowed to tell anyone," I reassured him.

She patted his shoulders. "Inside?"

"Come on in. You can play games on my phone while I work."

The games enticed him inside. I got Josh's arm set while he sat on the couch.

"I never got your name," I said, hating the awkwardness.

"Edith." She looked around, her eyes wide. "It's... cozy...in here."

"Yes, it's quite pleasant."

The decorations weren't overdone. Memphis had watercolor paintings of the woods and sunsets on the wall. I hadn't asked her if they were locally done, but the style matched the work hanging in the café. The earth tones of her furniture complemented the art. There was no clutter. Anywhere. Memphis wasn't a keeper of things.

Maverick's place would be busting at the seams after another year with Cricket.

Once Josh couldn't move his arm around as much, he settled into my phone.

Edith sat by his side, picking at a nail and craning her head all around, studying the kitchen and the hallway. "I didn't think there was anything to worry about. But then the dark circles appeared around his eyes."

I perched on the edge of the couch. "I've learned some things about shifters, but I haven't heard about the dark circles."

Her smile was friendly. "We can help, but only up to a point." Her gaze strayed to Josh, and she swallowed hard. "A lot of us die in car accidents. We can't call 9-1-1 and risk humans seeing us change. We can't go to a hospital. If the injuries are bad enough, we just...linger and succumb." The corners of her eyes pinched. "I was starting to get so scared."

"Have there been kids who..." Didn't recover. I wouldn't say it. I'd been around kids who looked like they weren't paying attention only to find out they could write a three-page dissertation breaking down the conversation adults thought they weren't listening to.

She waved off my question. "No. I mean, it's like old wives' tales."

So it did happen.

"I was afraid to come," she said sheepishly. "I'm just —it's Memphis. She's intimidating."

"What would Memphis have done?"

She gave me a quizzical look. "The healing power of the ruling family?" When I lifted a brow, she continued. "Healing? Rulers are supposed to be able to heal. I'm not sure about Maverick as her twin." She pressed her fingers to her forehead. "I could've gone to Maverick. He's much nicer."

"And Memphis is mean?" I'd seen her rip a head off. And she'd killed someone last night. But she didn't stomp through town yelling at innocent people. Usually, she was locked in her office working.

"No," she said quickly. "Sorry—I shouldn't have said anything."

"It's all right." I should learn the dynamics of my new home.

The door from the garage opened and Memphis

stepped in. She stopped as soon as her bright gaze landed on us. Her expression stayed impassive.

Edith rose, her hands clasped in front of her until her knuckles turned white. "Memphis. Apologies. Your mate is helping Josh. His arm wasn't mending."

A dark brow arched, and her gaze landed on the boy watching a show on my phone.

"He broke his arm and wasn't healing," Edith rushed on. "It was getting jostled and breaking all over again. Come on, Josh. Time to go. Memphis needs her house back."

Josh jerked his head up from my phone. "You said I wouldn't have to leave until it's healed."

"He wanted privacy," I explained.

"Josh." Edith crossed to him like she was going to yank him off the couch.

I held out a hand. "Wait. I need to evaluate his break and remove the bandages. How long does it take to mend a bone?"

Panic crossed Edith's face. Did Memphis do something to her? "We should go."

Memphis put her hand on the doorknob. "Josh needs to heal. Wait here until Vaughn clears him to go." She slipped out before either of us could say a word.

"She's going to hate me," Edith whispered.

"Has she given you a reason to think she dislikes you?"

"She punched my dad once," Josh announced from the couch.

I wasn't ready for that.

"Josh." She was scandalized. She gave me a you-know-what-it's-like smile. "Gordy was upset the city council wasn't giving him a liquor license to open a bar. He went to a meeting and she decked him."

My gut said I wasn't getting the whole story. "I can assure you when I treat patients, I'm only interested in their well-being. Any other drama stays out of the exam room." Until it didn't.

She pushed a lock of hair behind her ear. "We really should get going."

"Let me make you a cloth splint. It's not as rigid but will fit under his sleeve. He'll still have to be careful, but maybe it'll give him enough time to get the healing to stick." I looked over my shoulder. "Does that sound good, Josh?"

He stretched his arm. "I like the spoons. It's like a robot."

"They're Memphis's spoons," Edith stammered.

"I'm sure she'll be okay with it. Josh is part of her clan."

"Oh. Okay. Sure. We should go."

The female had been nervous from the moment I opened the door, but this was next level.

I was helpless to watch them scuttle out of the house. When they were gone, I waited another hour, but Memphis didn't return. My stomach rumbled, and I went to the kitchen. Burritos were in the fridge.

After holding her in the tub, I'd say we'd moved beyond my boycott of her thoughtful gestures. I heated the food up and ate. Outside, the light faded. Memphis didn't come home.

Why would she stay gone so long? Surely she didn't hold me treating a patient under her roof against me? It was my roof too.

I roamed the house. The last thing I wanted to do was

close myself into that damn office. Maybe it was being able to treat a patient hands-on, but I grabbed a light coat and left.

The walk to city hall took minutes. The light where her office was shone alone in the dark building. The main door was unlocked, but apparently, Memphis's reputation was enough to keep intruders away.

I found her at her desk, her feet kicked up, watching her computer screen. I marched in and pressed my fingertips to the desktop.

Without looking, she asked, "How's your patient?"

I couldn't tell from her tone how she felt. But she was avoiding the house. Maybe me. The Vaughn from two days ago might've been fine about it. Today's Vaughn wasn't. "The patient is out of the house, yes."

Her mouth tightened like she wasn't happy with my answer. "Is he okay?"

"Should be."

She paused, waiting for more. Her lips thinning, she said, "I'm concerned about one of my people."

"And I'm used to confidentiality. Why aren't you home?"

She still didn't do more than glance at me. The show she was watching was some black-and-white flick I didn't recognize but was something I wouldn't have pegged as Memphis's taste. "I'm sure Edith filled you in."

"Barely, and only from her point of view."

Her gaze finally slid to me and stuck. "Her mate deserved more than to get decked. He directly challenged me."

"Isn't that what that one lady did when I arrived in town?"

"Yes, but she'd been manipulating the clan for years

to take over, making her a danger to the clan. Edith's mate is a blustering oaf with an anger problem who questioned my authority."

My doctor brain got stuck on the anger issue. "Do you think he was the one who kept hurting Josh so he couldn't heal?"

She frowned. "I don't know. Our kind experiences domestic disputes and abuse, but it's not as reported."

"And if it is, then what?"

"Edith is the first line of defense for her family. Then other family members. Then Maverick and I will step in."

"Termination?"

Her expression was tight. "It depends."

"You'll kill a man for eating cattle that's not his but—"

Her boots slammed to the floor. "I don't like it either. The feral shifter threatens all our kind. An abusive dad is an asshole and needs to be punished, but like it or not, that's how our laws are. Termination for not following our laws, for threatening our people. You want the dad dead? Go kill him."

I fisted my hands together. She deliberately made it so I'd instantly reject the violence. But I couldn't stand by and let a kid get hurt—if that was what was going on. I also wasn't going to get help from her. After I'd come to her aid last night.

I'd never understand these people. "I'll be sleeping in the office tonight. So you can come home if you're here to avoid me." I stalked out.

This morning, I wondered if I had a future here. I still didn't have answers.

emphis

I WOKE TO KNOCKING. I scrubbed my hands over my face and blinked at Maverick in the doorway. "Is it morning already?"

His disappointed gaze rested on me. "I thought you made some progress with Vaughn."

"Roll that progress right back." I dropped my feet down from the desk and unkinked my neck. I stood and stretched. "Still have that overnight kit in your office?"

When he'd get kicked out of his home by his ex, he'd sleep here and clean up in the old locker room until he and Astra were on again. So glad each of them had found a mate who fit them.

"I happily tossed it when Astra got mated. If I had one now, it'd be a him-and-hers kit because I'd keep Cricket here all night for *reasons.*"

"Ugh, you two are disgusting."

"Thoroughly. Go home. It's your house and you can't have the town talking about how you're sleeping under separate roofs."

Probably too late for that. "I didn't mean to. He came here upset, and we got into an argument, and he left. I sat thinking about stuff and drifted off." I'd been more tired than I thought from the night before.

"What was the problem?"

I should've known he'd pry. I lifted my chin toward the door. After he closed it, I settled back into my chair, then popped up again. My ass did not want to see that seat for a while.

Pacing the office, I described the situation. "Edith brought Josh by because his arm wasn't mending."

"How could that be?"

"He refused to give specifics. Patient doctor confidentiality." Or stubbornness. Everything that happened in the clan was my business.

"How could a kid not heal from a broken arm? Unless someone keeps messing with it." His eyes widened, almost like looking into a mirror.

"I don't like Josh's dad. Hell, it could be Edith, for all I know. Vaughn lost his shit when he learned there might not be a lot I can do about an abuser when he's known me to kill two others since he's been here." I let that sink in. The reality had weighed on my mind for hours. Shifters gave as good as they got, but there were still imbalances of power. I couldn't see Edith standing up to a blustering Gordy. He towered over her and his anger was like a flash-bang bomb. Instant and loud.

I continued to pace. "Vaughn's right. It's fucked up."

"Yeah, it is. But I can't see Levi or me becoming a police officer like Steel Silver in Silver Lake."

No, but that'd be useful. We were slowly growing and would need to do more for local law enforcement since it wasn't like we could imprison a shifter. One shift under that kind of surveillance and our secret would be out. Peridot Fall's tiny fire department was all volunteer, and while they had some experience fighting fires and responding to crashes, they were woefully undertrained.

"I'll keep thinking on it, but we also have to find out if Josh is in an abusive home and since Edith shakes in her booties when I'm around, it won't be me finding out."

"We need to take the bigger issue to the council." When I nodded, he waved me out of the office. "Go home. Clean up. Make a show of it so everyone thinks you were working late."

"It shouldn't matter," I grumbled as I walked out.

"But it does," he called after me.

I walked home, enjoying the crisp fall air. Snow would come soon enough. I liked all the seasons, but after the last day and night I'd had, the slap in the face by the wind was welcome.

Without bothering to muffle my movements, I entered my home like I owned the place. I did. I wouldn't creep around Vaughn. We already had a communication problem.

I went to the fridge to grab the breakfast burritos I made yesterday, only to find the spot empty. Confused, I checked the trash, but they weren't there either. A single plate was cleaned and set in the drying rack.

If he'd eaten them, it was likely before Edith and Josh's visit.

The door to Vaughn's room was closed and his voice

drifted through. I went to the bathroom and washed up. His talking had ceased by the time I was done and went to my bedroom. I closed and changed into fresh clothing —jeans and a black T-shirt with a flannel over it. I was finger-combing my hair when I opened the door to find Vaughn waiting in the hallway.

I jumped—very uncharacteristic of me. "How the hell didn't I hear you?"

He didn't smile, and his expression was unreadable. "I can be quiet when I want to."

That he'd snuck up on me on purpose should be concerning, but I found it sexy. Challenging. So many people in town didn't know what to do around me. Maverick was the charming one. Levi was approachable. I was the scary ruler. Edith's reaction was exaggerated, but how I felt like everyone acted around me.

"I need to go to Minneapolis," he said, shoving his hands in his slacks. "For a week. It's going to be a regular occurrence."

How convenient. "Sure."

"You don't believe me?"

"I believe you want to leave for a week."

"I want to be allowed to do my job."

I prickled at his defensiveness. "What's it like to pick the career you want to do?"

His lips flattened. My message was loud and clear. "What's it like to be able to do your job without inter-ference?"

"Is that how you'd describe it?"

He shook his head like he was shaking off water. "Edith was nervous in this house."

"It's not hers."

"It's not mine either."

"No, you had to give yours up when I made you move." I was suddenly weary. Tired of everything. Sick of my role in the clan but determined to do my people justice. "Here's the thing, Vaughn—we don't break limbs easily. We heal faster, but we're also stronger than humans. Our injuries tend to be more of the soft tissue variety. Our deaths occur from bleeding out. Major trauma does the trick, things like planes, trains, and automobiles. We can't outmuscle a car rolling on top of us. A fall. A broken arm that *for some reason* didn't heal would take weeks, probably months, to drain the energy of the shifter."

His frown deepened with each point I made. "I don't get why she'd come to your house if she was scared of her husband—mate. Unless she wanted us to figure it out?"

"Gordy is a blustering oaf with a hair-trigger temper. Edith is a timid mouse, but she's still a shifter. Rebellion against the controlling male in the relationship? She might've come out of sincere worry for her kid as a fuck you to Gordy. I don't know."

"Josh said you had to punch him?"

My reputation preceded me once again. "To put him in his place. He said only a fool would think he was a fool and that the council must be full of idiots to turn down his liquor license."

"A verbal tongue-lashing wouldn't do?"

"Not in our world." He nodded like he understood, and relief flowed through me. "If there's a problem at home, she isn't going to tell me. Look how nervous she was yesterday."

"She was. Josh was chill though." He pushed a hand through his hair.

So much of this wasn't making sense. "Was his arm broken?"

"Without an X-ray, there's no way to be certain. He treated his limb like it hurt. Pointed out where it hurt and had a plausible story. He didn't react as if he was in great pain, but I chalked it up to being a shifter."

Partly accurate. We felt just as much pain as a human, but it didn't last as long.

Vaughn's distressed expression deepened. "Would they play us—me? Why?"

"I don't know. But while you're gone, that's what I'll be working on." I made another point with my tone.

He shoved a hand through his hair and checked his watch. "Shit, I have a call in a few minutes."

"Don't let me interfere more than I have." I sidled around him and went to my bedroom, shutting the door behind me. My gaze fell on the unmade bed from yesterday when I'd woken up next to him. Not sure when that'd happen again.

THE NORMAL WORKDAY WAS DONE, and everyone was leaving city hall. I stared out my office window at the fading sunlight. It didn't matter when I left. There was no one to miss me at home.

Vaughn had been out of town all week. Without him under the roof, I should've had a better night's sleep than when he was brooding in his office. Instead, I slept fitfully, dreaming of what he would've kept doing to my nipple and how he could've taken it further—worse, how I would've let him.

My body was on fire and there was a throbbing

between my thighs that refused to go away. Since he was gone, I made judicial use of solitude to get myself off, but solo orgasms almost made it worse. Because when I was about to come, it was his flashing eyes I pictured moving over me. His long fingers inside me instead of mine. His cock getting me off instead of a toy.

He was supposed to be back tonight or tomorrow. I needed to get at least one more round of solo playtime in before he got home.

There was a knock at the door. I didn't have to look to sense Maverick.

"Come on, Levi and I are taking you out."

My lust ebbed but never went away. Damn shifters and their high libidos. I was used to going for long periods between sex, and since I'd never had a guy who could tolerate me or my life for long, I was also used to a sporadic sex life. Must be the mating bond. My natural shifter hormones were demanding fulfillment. I stuffed it all away.

"It's like it's my birthday or something," I said wryly and swiveled around.

His mouth tipped up. "Thanks for the tickets to Vegas. You didn't have to. Now it's my turn to give you your birthday present."

I never paid attention to my birthday. Sharing it with Maverick meant I got to ride on his celebratory coattails. When he was dating his ex, he and I would have lunch and then he'd do his thing. Sometimes I'd go to the city to find some company for the night. Now the only company I could have was in the city, avoiding me.

I rose. My hunger wasn't as strong as my desire, but a meal with my brothers was a nice distraction. "Mm, a cheeseburger totally trumps plane tickets."

He grinned. "It's your birthday. I'll buy you two cheeseburgers."

I walked out with him. "It's our birthday. Levi's buying the meal."

When he entered the café, only Levi was sitting in a booth. The bakery had closed hours ago, but it was just him. "Where's Cricket and Briony?"

"They're coming later." He lifted his chin toward the other side of the booth. "Sit."

The older sister in me wanted to challenge his bossiness, but I tamped it down. He wasn't one to throw orders around. When I settled and Maverick slid across from him, Levi pushed an envelope across the table.

"Happy Birthday," he said.

I glanced at each of them. "Is this an intervention? I know I work a lot, but seriously, it's not a problem—"

"Memphis—open the damn gift." Maverick was exasperated.

A gift? Curious, I peeled the seal open and slipped out a piece of paper. I scanned the contents. "An itinerary?" Laughter burst out of me. "You got me tickets to Vegas too?"

Maverick grinned. "Twin thinking. Yes. These are for you to get away."

I squinted at the date. The tickets I'd gotten him were for the holidays when the weather in Las Vegas would be a lot nicer than here. "The flight is tomorrow?"

"It's been a shit month—year—for you," Levi said. "Get away. Relax. Have some fun."

"The hotel room has a whirlpool tub?" I frowned. I hadn't gone outside of the state unless I drove to the other clans in North Dakota, and the dates for the room went until next weekend. "I can't be gone that long."

Maverick and Levi exchanged an *I knew it* look.

"Yes, you can," Maverick said. "Both of us are here. We can spy on Gordy, and you can relax for a few days."

I didn't mention Vaughn was coming back tonight. Or tomorrow. He hadn't been clear.

As if he'd read my mind, Maverick gave me an understanding look. "Just go. You deserve it."

"It'll look bad," I said.

Levi shook his head. "If he can go out of town for a week for work, so can you."

I rolled my eyes, but I appreciated his support. "That's different."

"It's no one's business," Maverick said. "I'll tell the council I thought it'd be better for your fertility to relax a bit."

I wrinkled my nose. "I guess if I have to endure you and a bunch of elders talking about my fertility, I might as well be eating at fancy restaurants and soaking in a hot tub."

"If Vaughn gets back after you go, we'll talk to him." Maverick lifted a shoulder. "Cricket will gladly talk to him —gleefully rub it in—but I might steal the joy and do it myself."

My brothers were irritated at Vaughn, not because he left for work but because he'd reverted to his old self after one setback. They were salty about his job since he hid behind it, but I did the same. Cricket rallied for me, and I hadn't expected her support. But she probably wanted everyone else to be as deliriously in love as her.

She'd have to keep dreaming when it came to Vaughn and me.

I tucked the itinerary away. Maverick and Levi sent me all the details. All I had to do was pack and go.

After we finished eating and Levi picked up the tab, I walked straight to my house. Now that my brothers weren't around, my thoughts strayed to soaking in a hot tub and what it might be like to have Vaughn's soapy hands running over my body.

When I reached home, I was relieved to see the driveway empty. I could've gone to the office, but then my brothers might've stopped in to check on me. I didn't want to be caught stroking one off behind my desk.

The thrum between my legs was driving me crazy and I needed a quick release. I'd take a bath, daydream while I climaxed, and maybe I'd sleep decently tonight. Stripping down in my bedroom, I carried my nightshirt to the bathroom. I doubted Vaughn would drive back tonight. It wasn't like there was anything here he wanted.

CHAPTER

SIX

I PARKED in the driveway and stared at the closed garage door. I wasn't directly behind Memphis's pickup. The week in the city hadn't been the getaway I'd hoped for. I thought I'd be consumed by work, too busy to think about the sexy female in the house I shouldn't want so badly.

Each day had been filled with meetings. I got to see some patients in person and that would help me treat them with telemedicine. I met my boss, my colleagues, and the evening social had been barely tolerable.

I'd been hit on by my two coworkers—a fellow physician and a nurse practitioner. Each night we went out to eat as a group and each night, I got an invite back to a hotel room.

Each night, I went to my own hotel room, uninter-

69

ested but with a raging erection. All those women did was make me remember Memphis's lithe naked body and how warm and tight her nipple had been. I managed to politely turn them down without telling them to fuck off outright like I wanted to.

My dick was almost raw from the many times I'd stroked off. Being away from her was somehow worse.

Sighing, I glanced at the house. A light was on farther in. Probably her bedroom light, and if it was, then she was in the bathroom. It was like she didn't want to come out of the bathroom to a dark house.

As much as I'd stroked off to her, I wasn't ready to face her. Definitely not a freshly bathed Memphis that smelled like dessert.

Going inside, I quietly closed the car door, leaving my suitcase in the back of my car to deal with tomorrow. I could be a jackass for one more day and sneak into the office. Maybe I could get some actual rest. Memphis would realize I was home and would know by the closed office door I didn't want to visit. She probably didn't want to see me back. The time I was gone must've been refreshing, downright relaxing, not to have my moody ass hanging around.

Easing through the garage door, I silently closed it behind me. Just as I was about to take a step, I thought I heard a whimper. Cocking my head, I listened harder.

A moan.

Was she okay? Did something happen again while I was gone?

Pissed at myself for leaving her alone to deal with it all herself, I toed my shoes off in case I had to crawl into the tub again.

Only the next moan was different. It was *that* kind of noise.

My dick instantly turned to concrete, pushing at my zipper.

No. It couldn't be.

I stopped outside the bathroom door. There it was. A breathy gasp.

For fuck's sake, was that what she sounded like? I squeezed my eyes shut. My erection throbbed. The caveman inside of me told me to bang down the door and take my woman.

A hiss and a gasp. The shower was running into what sounded like a full tub. The shower wand.

Christ, I didn't realize what the device could be used for. How obtuse could I be?

I rested my forearms on the door frame and listened. Maybe I shouldn't be a pervert, but nothing would pry me away from the auditory mindfuck I was getting.

Her moan increased in volume, turning into a cry that faded.

What the hell?

Was that all? I could do better than that. I could make her scream my name until she lost her voice. I could bury my face so far between her legs she wouldn't quit coming until the sun lit the horizon. And then I'd drive into her—

My body trembled. It was like I could feel her soaked skin against my lips. Her powerful thighs wrapped around my head and then my waist. She was so fucking strong she'd kill my dick, and I'd have the most magnificent death and beg for her to do it again.

I was panting like a bull when the door flung open.

"Oh my god!" Her eyes were wide, her sweet red lips

parted, and she couldn't look more shocked and horrified.

She was right there. Nothing but a towel wrapped around her body. My pesky slacks could disintegrate into dust for all I cared. I'd rip these bastards off so fast they'd combust.

My chest was heaving. The pain from my erection clouded my mind. I was nothing but the beast I thought this town was full of. I wanted to fall on her, ravage her, just get some fucking relief.

The week without her was torture, but seeing her in front of me, cheeks pink from a hot bath and a climax—I wasn't a strong man right now.

She deserved better than a mindless rutting creature, and after the way I treated her, she definitely deserved wine and flowers first.

Wheezing in a heavy breath, I pushed off the door frame. "I'm home." And then I stalked to the office and shut my horny self inside so she didn't have to deal with me.

I CRACKED AN EYE OPEN. Yep. My dick was still hard.

I drifted into a crap sleep with her moans in my ears. I couldn't bring myself to jack off after I'd eavesdropped on her. Control wasn't completely out of my grasp.

Rolling over with a groan, I winced at my stiff back and neck. I'd been spoiled sleeping on a bed the last week.

The sound of the garage door opening reached me. Frowning, I rose and adjusted my slacks around my perma-erection. Her truck fired up, and the engine faded in the distance, the garage door shutting.

Where was she going? She walked everywhere. At night, she flew.

A thought that was getting more normal.

I should get moving for the day. I'd have to get my suitcase out of my car. Unpack. Wash clothes. First, I needed a shower. Since she was gone and it'd been a good six hours since I'd heard her orgasm, I wouldn't feel like such a lech if I stroked one out in the shower.

I'd need to come ten times to get rid of this hard-on.

Once the shower was done, I dressed in another pair of slacks and a shirt. I didn't have to work today, but my clothing stabilized me. I was physically the same. Mentally, I was struggling. I went to the kitchen to look for food. No burritos were waiting for me.

Had she taken time to eat before she left? Maybe she left to grab some food. The fridge was unusually empty.

There was a knock at the door. I pushed away and answered, hoping there was no kid with possibly one abusive parent on the other side. No kid. No parent. Cricket was on the front step, her arms folded, her expression furious, and her fingers tapping on her gray knit sweater.

"Bug, hey. Long time no s—"

"I can't believe you just let her go."

"Let who go?"

She looked to the sky like she had had enough of me. Usually, our roles were reversed. I wasn't used to being chastised by my sister, but the occurrences were getting more frequent the longer I was in Peridot Falls.

"Memphis. On vacation."

Confusion was crowded out by alarm. "What vacation?"

"Haven't you talked to her since you've been back?"

The image of her in the towel flashed through my mind. Technically, I had talked. "Not really. I got back late."

Cricket narrowed her eyes, calling me on my bullshit. "The guys got her a Vegas vacation for her birthday." When she saw my stunned expression, her eyes widened. "You didn't know it was her birthday yesterday?"

"I…" Had no excuse. My first silly thought was *she had birthdays?* "Shit."

"Yeah. Shit."

"She's going to Vegas?"

Cricket nodded. "She's on her way to the airport in Minneapolis."

Fuck. "For how long?"

"Through next weekend. Mav and Levi wanted to give her some nice time off after the rough six months she's had."

I couldn't feel more like a festering pile of shit. My eyelids drifted shut. She didn't deserve me. But I could keep ignoring her, locking myself in my office, getting upset when her job and this life frustrated me, or I could be a man and face how I really felt. "Where's she staying?"

Cricket kicked a hip out. The cunning expression was new. The woman Cricket had become since meeting Maverick and moving to this small shifter town was more confident and relaxed than the girl I raised in Las Vegas.

"Good thing I made sure they booked two tickets just in case you two would want to go together." She lifted a shoulder. "Levi said it was a long shot."

Levi hadn't grown up in a gambling town. My sister and I had. She'd bet on me, and I wouldn't let her down. "Give me all the details."

Memphis

I WAS BUCKLED into first class. The stream of people had quit coming through the door and the plane would take off soon. I hadn't traveled a lot and the airport ordeal was interesting, but I made it. My carry-on was stored and—bonus—I had an empty seat next to me along with all the extra room in first class.

My brothers were the best.

Flight attendants roamed up and down the aisle. I had my tablet loaded with books. The flight wouldn't take long, but I was looking forward to not needing to do anything but sit in this chair and veg out.

A familiar peppery-amber scent washed over me, and I looked up just as a scowling shadow fell over me.

"Vaughn?" His name was out of my mouth as I was

trying to figure out who I was seeing and why he was there.

He was breathing heavily just as an attendant stopped next to him and asked to store his carry-on. He jerked a shopping bag from his suitcase and gave the attendant a curt nod of thanks.

"What are you—" My brothers. The empty spot next to me wasn't a coincidence in an otherwise full flight. "Why are you here?"

He slid into the seat and handed the bag over. "I didn't realize it was your birthday yesterday." He waved his hand at the bundle. "Sorry for the wrapping, but I didn't have much notice about what was going on."

I cradled the...gift? Peeling the bag open, my gaze landed on books. Vaughn was watching me. The attendant stopped again. "Sir, can you buckle up, please?"

"Yeah," he said without looking at her. He found his seat belt and buckled, all while watching me take each book out, look at the cover, and read the back.

Romances. All of them.

He cleared his throat like he was nervous about speaking. "I, uh, thought with your job you'd like something light-hearted with a happy ending. I stayed away from the paranormal aspects. For obvious reasons. But since you were watching *Roman Holiday* in your office, I thought maybe you liked light romance books too."

Getting a gift from him left me speechless as it was, but each book he'd picked out was one I'd looked at while waiting for boarding to begin. I turned over one of the brightly covered books and flipped it back again.

"Shit, you hate them."

"No." I stuffed two of them into the bag and left out

the one I'd been the most interested in. "You put some thought into the purchase."

"That surprises you?" He shook his head. "Stupid question."

"Why are you here?"

"You're going to Las Vegas for a vacation."

I pursed my lips. Did my brothers pick the location on purpose? It was an easy trip from Minneapolis and had all the amenities I could want. Vegas was also Vaughn's hometown. "My brothers picked it."

"I would've joined you. Even if it wasn't Vegas."

"Why?" I laughed, the bitterness drawing the attention of the passengers across from us. "You've been out of town and didn't say more than one sentence to me when you returned. You bolted yourself into your room and avoided me all morning."

The muscle in Vaughn's cheek jumped and he scanned the plane. The safety briefing started, and I should probably listen, but I couldn't take my gaze off him. His hair looked like he'd done little more than finger-comb it. He was in a rumpled pin-striped shirt and charcoal-gray slacks. I had no way of knowing other than intuition, but I didn't think he often left the house looking this rumpled.

Then he leaned close. "One, I slept like shit and didn't hear anything until you were driving away. And two, you got one sentence from me because I was trying not to ravage you like a horny beast."

The plane started to move, but my world stopped. "You heard that," I squeaked, flustered but seriously turned on.

When I'd found him outside the bathroom door, I'd been mortified. I had come a whisper away from calling his name as I climaxed. I thought I'd diverted a catastrophe. He'd been looking at me like I was the worst thing that could've ever happened to him.

I'd been sure he hadn't heard me finishing myself off.

While I was too stunned to speak, he dropped his head farther down to murmur in my ear. "After hearing your needy moans, all I could think about was getting my mouth on that hot little clit of yours."

I did the weakest wiggle, anything to get rid of that incessant throb, and his gaze tracked down to my lap.

"I heard it all, Memphis. How many times did you get yourself off while I was away?"

"Not enough and too many," I whispered.

"Same." He took the bag of books from my hands and set them over his lap to help conceal the bulge he was sporting. "You deserve better from me. When we get to Las Vegas, I'll take you on a proper date. And we'll see how it goes from there."

Yes, please screamed through my brain, but I couldn't say it. He'd been an ass for a reason, but I wanted more out of a relationship. I'd resigned myself to having a mate who didn't like me. Making babies with a guy who wished for a different mother for his kids. Yet the longer I was with him, the less willing I was to capitulate so easily. I wanted a mate who respected me, if nothing else.

I could turn him down for the date. Make him do more than buy books I was absolutely interested in—my twin wouldn't have even picked out better options. But he was here, in the seat next to me, and for now, that was a start.

Vaughn

I opened the hotel room door and froze. The lady at the desk had rattled off the information, but nothing had clicked until now. One bed.

A king-size bed was the masterpiece of the room, with a large window spanning the length and a hot tub by the view. A honeymoon suite. The fuckers.

There was a couch that would be hell on my back to sleep on, but it was time to be honest with myself. I wanted to be done with floors and couches and chairs. There was no greater demand pounding me than sleeping in the same bed as Memphis—except for getting inside her.

"You can use the bathroom first," Memphis said as she pushed past me. She must've already prepared herself for the situation. Perhaps she even assumed I'd take the couch or doze in the empty hot tub rather than crawl onto the same mattress as her. "Our reservations are in an hour, but from the itinerary, it looks like the restaurant is in the hotel."

I went in and let the door shut behind me. She stopped at the windows and gazed out. We were several stories up. The whole city was laid out like it was on display just for her.

"You can get ready first," I said. A shower was my top priority. After traveling yesterday and sleeping so poorly, I needed to clean up and shave.

"I'd like to stretch out for a minute." Lights from the city gleamed along her dark hair as she looked from side to side.

"First time in Vegas?"

"First time flying anywhere. First time in a city bigger than the Twin Cities."

She said it so casually I almost missed the significance. "You've never traveled before?"

What I had thought was a cool aloofness toward me while we walked through the airport was her reading signs and following directions.

"Road trips mostly. Camping."

"I've always liked the skyline," I blurted, and she cocked a brow over her shoulder. "It's different than other cities. Unique. There's no other place like Las Vegas."

The corner of her mouth tipped up, and she went to staring back out the window.

I found the luggage rack. Situating the suitcase I'd left in the car last night, I dug out my shower bag and disappeared into the spacious bathroom. It was four times the size of her house's bathroom, with a soaking tub, a walk-in shower, and a double sink with a floor-to-ceiling closet.

The only thing I concentrated on while showering was not nicking myself shaving. I kept the towel around my waist when I left the bathroom. Nerves banged outside the door of my calm. Tonight's date meant more than any other I'd been on. It was hard not to feel like my future hinged on this date.

"The restaurant—is it fancy?" I asked. What would her brothers book her? She wasn't the cocktail dress type, but then she'd probably never needed one. Peridot Falls didn't have black tie events.

"Dress nice was all the directions said."

"Cool."

Her smile was faint as she ducked into the bathroom, rolling her black hard-bodied suitcase behind her.

I'd had my clothing dry-cleaned while I was in Minneapolis for work. Since I hadn't unpacked, I would have all I needed and a few extra wrinkles. Once I was dressed, I paced the room, straightening my tie and tugging on the sleeves of my slate-gray suit coat. My shirt underneath was pale pink, and it'd earned gushy compliments from one of my colleagues. So I'd only worn it once last week.

The door opened.

I turned to ask if she was ready, but my tongue stuck to the roof of my mouth. I had to stop pacing and control myself before I became the panting beast from last night.

Her dress was just shy of formal. A deep forest green that reminded me of the color on her dragon scales underneath the vivid peridot. One side was sleeveless, the other a gauzy covering in the same material as her skirt. A slit up the side of her thigh let the material swirl around her legs and tease the eye with tanned, firm flesh.

Her hair was a flirty swirl around her head. It'd grown a couple inches since I'd arrived. The sides were now long enough to slick back while the silky hair on top of her head fell over it.

She was barefoot as she rolled her suitcase out.

"Don't worry," she said, going to the other side of the bed. "I don't have combat boots to pair with this."

"I think you'd look great in them. You do look great. Beautiful." Sexy. Stunning. So damn fuckable I wasn't sure how I could be decent in public.

She bent to put shoes on and when she straightened, she was taller.

I groaned. "You have heels?"

She paused, coming around the bed. "Yeah. Why?" She glanced down at herself. "Do I look awkward?"

I pulled the crotch of my ever-tightening trousers down. Fuck me. How was I going to survive tonight? The hint of uncertainty in her expression was my undoing. "I'm struggling here, Memphis. All I want to do is bend you over the bed and sink into you. I want to thrust until I have no more orgasms to give or get. I want to fuck you until the sun rises and neither of us can walk straight."

Her sweet lips parted. "Oh." She glanced around.

I swallowed hard, reining in my lust as much as I could. I cocked my elbow out. "But my lady is getting her fancy birthday dinner, so I'll control myself."

She licked her tongue across her lower lip. Did she have gloss on? I was toast. I was going to incinerate myself during our meal. She walked toward me, the heels giving her a different sway to her hips, as mesmerizing as her regular walk.

Slipping her hand through my arm, she gave me a hesitant smile. I led her out the door and to the elevator bank. She tapped a toe, and when we got inside an empty elevator, she patted her thigh. My usually quiet and stealthy dragon shifter was fidgety.

"Are you nervous?" I asked.

I thought she'd deny it, but she sighed. "Is it that obvious? I'm going to fuck this up. It's like leading a bull through a porcelain aisle."

"Have you ever seen a Texas longhorn get out of a trailer?" When she turned her incredulous gaze toward me, I winced. "I'm not good with women, believe it or not. I wasn't comparing you to a bull." That got her to relax. "What I mean is, I've seen some videos of them. They step out, very aware of their horns and how not to catch them on the edges. So I think if you lead a bull through an aisle full of breakables, he'd probably surprise you. Because even outside their element, they're aware of themselves. I'm not a rancher, but a lot of my new patients are country kids and they talk about their dairy cattle and farm animals—and send me those videos to watch. They say bulls run fast and can sneak up on you. It's when they're scared they get erratic. We're all like that. You're not a bull or a cow. You're fucking sexy, and I don't care if you eat with your hands tonight."

That could've gone better.

"Shit, Vaughn."

The doors dinged open and I gestured for her to exit. "Ladies first."

A simple saying, but her demeanor changed to shyness. Aware. I was seeing a side of Memphis no one else ever had. Feminine. Soft. Not just a dragon shifter or a female. She was strong but delicate.

I would make sure I handled her with care.

VAUGHN'S WORDS echoed through my head. Between what he'd said in the hotel room and then on the elevator ride, my mind was spinning. I was caught in the middle of wanting to be inside my head and mull over everything he'd said and done today or gawking at the bright lights, the crush of people, and the differences between this one place and my entire town.

We were seated in a partially secluded circular booth. Other than the waiter popping in and out, it was a lot like we had the place to ourselves.

Since Vaughn had soothed my nerves in the elevator, I tapped my finger on a cool fork. "I looked all these up, but do people really use all this silverware?"

His smile was kind. I sensed no mocking attitude coming off him. "You looked it up?"

I nodded. "The airport. What to expect in first class. The hotel. Fine dining." I could recite Las Vegas's tourism facts. "That's what I did last night and before I packed this morning."

"Yes, to the silverware, but the waiter won't police you if you use your salad fork for the chicken parmesan."

We shared a quick grin, and it increased the intimacy of the moment.

"You really are beautiful," he murmured.

Unsure how to take his compliment, I ran my fingers along the edge of the cloth napkin. "Thanks."

"I've always thought so. You're stunning."

"God, Vaughn. I don't know what to do with you."

"What do you mean?"

I swept my hand over the table. "This. And you. It's fucking with my head. I thought we had some sort of progress that night in the tub and then when you came to my office and abruptly left town..."

"The trip was truly last minute." A line formed between his reddish-brown brows. "I was hit on twice while I was gone."

The urge to change into my dragon and rampage down the Strip was strong, but I wasn't a mindless creature. A bigger part of me than I cared to acknowledge had wondered if he'd be with someone else while he was gone.

I eked out a nonchalant "Oh?"

"They were straightforward. Asked me to their hotel rooms. One even said she loved this shirt with this suit. Said the pink complemented the gray."

The bitch was right. Damn her. He looked sharp in his outfit. Devastating. I wanted to peel every piece off. But right now, I was caught between the need to scream and weep, and I didn't like the feeling. I didn't do jealousy. I hated this sense of inadequacy and being surrounded by opulence only magnified the emotions.

"I never wore the suit again. Had it cleaned and packed it. I went to my room each night, alone, and although I didn't entertain the idea of sleeping with them, I got real fucking nauseous when they asked."

Relief was like a snowball to the face. "Yeah?"

"Yeah. I'm also feeling pretty cocky right now because you got a lot of looks on the way here, and I'm the lucky bastard who gets to be with you."

"I still don't—"

He leaned over and captured my mouth. The hard kiss turned sensual in a heartbeat, and his tongue was coaxing my mouth open. I stroked my tongue along his. The dry but sweet flavor of the champagne we'd been served tasted better on him.

A throat cleared, and I tensed, but Vaughn didn't yank himself away. He rested his thumb and forefinger on my chin, softly broke the kiss, and faced the waiter, his gaze expectant.

The waiter acted like there was nothing amiss and maybe for him, it was a tame night.

I stumbled through ordering, but then Vaughn would add his recommendations, and his sincere tone powered me through. I was getting some sort of steak and salad, and I didn't care about the rest.

Vaughn was a wall of heat next to me. I turned my head, and he was there, his face inches away. He might've kissed me, but that didn't clear anything up. "Is this a 'what stays in Vegas' thing?"

His eyes darkened like he didn't like the thought he might be leading me on and then would be back to Office

Vaughn when we got home. "I'm very attracted to you." His intense gaze speared mine. "Always have been."

"Always?" I chuckled, thinking of all the times he'd seen me. Dripping in another shifter's blood. Every day dressed like I was ready to drive a semi cross-country or head out to my lumberjack job—on my motorcycle. I didn't usually care, but I knew I wasn't Vaughn's type.

"Since the beginning," he affirmed. "I think that's why it's been so hard for me. I can't distance myself, no matter how hard I try."

I nodded and dropped my attention to the bubbles floating up in my flute glass.

"I don't want to stay apart from you. There's something between us. Something I've never felt with anyone." His smile was small, almost teasing. "I'm sure an uptight guy isn't your type."

He'd been my type since we'd met. But I knew what he meant, and he was right. "The guys I've been with are usually rougher around the edges."

The darkness was back in his eyes. "Anyone serious in your past?"

I snorted. "Surprisingly, not many males lined up to be second fiddle in the relationship. My work has to come first. Even before me."

He handed me my glass of champagne and grabbed his. "You've been looking in the wrong spots. There's nothing wrong with having a strong partner, no matter the gender. That was never my issue with you. *You* were never my issue with you unless you count how badly I want to fuck you."

A kick of desire hit my gut, squirmed in, and sank lower. I wanted this man too.

"It's a new and shocking world. But I've come to

understand your responsibilities. Not many could handle the weight."

The only other choice was to dump the role on my brothers.

The various parts of our meal showed up, and the night turned into the most unique date I'd ever had. Admittedly, not a hard task, but we swapped bites to taste each other's dishes and talked about the food and the experience. Then he started guessing the backstories of the couples around us.

Vaughn took a bite of asparagus and glanced at the couple three booths down. "He's an elementary school-teacher and his partner is a CEO. It's their fifth anniversary, and he wants to propose."

"No, the guy you think is the teacher is the CEO—of a tech company. The guy in the suit is the teacher."

"I'll accept that story." He glanced at an older couple, two booths in the opposite direction. "Fortieth anniversary. Kids are grown. They go south for the winter every year and stop in Vegas on their way."

I eyed the way the couple was sitting close to us. Both the man and woman were similar in age and they were Velcroed to each other. I was going to guess a second marriage, but scratch that. Their movements were stiff, almost a put-on. "They're on the brink of divorce. This is their last hoorah, but they've each made their decision, and when they get home, they'll file. I'd say they each have a lawyer with papers who's ready at the word go."

"Shit." Vaughn gave them one last stare. "That's depressing. How'd you know?"

"Since I rarely leave Peridot Falls?" I smiled at his guilty look. "I watch a lot of TV. Hollywood gets a lot of things wrong, but they get a lot right too. Small towns have drama too."

The rest of our food arrived. After we were done with dessert, I pushed the plate away. Another bottle of champagne was delivered.

"Do shifters get drunk?"

"If we drink enough, quickly, but it doesn't last long. The healing works the same. Eventually the system will tire of healing the damage the alcohol does to someone who has a drinking problem. They'll perish earlier."

He poured me another glass but left his dry. "I don't want to be tanked now that I get to enjoy you." He put his mouth close to my ear and his hot breath wafted across my skin. So damn good. "Do you want that?"

"Yes," I breathed.

He trailed his hand over my thigh, pushing the edge of my dress as he went.

"I can't forget how soft your skin is." He turned me toward him. The tablecloth was draped over our legs, and from the outside, we looked like a cozy couple. But his hand disappeared under my skirt and I wasn't stopping him. Instead, I widened my legs.

His fingers trailed along the bare skin between my thighs, and he groaned. "Fuck, Memphis. No underwear?"

"I didn't want lines," I whispered.

"You're going to kill me in all the best ways. Now put your hands on the table like a good girl and let me sink my fingers into you."

Fire ripped underneath my skin. I wanted to be a good girl for him. I wanted someone else in charge. I put my palms on the tablecloth and casually looked around us. The other diners were minding their own business.

And then his fingertips hit my clit.

He brought his mouth close to my ear again. "You're fucking soaked."

"I should've worn underwear," I hissed. I didn't think I'd have his fingers tunneling their way inside me. My world tilted and the only thing that kept me upright was him. He pressed closer to me and changed the position of his hand.

"Vaughn."

"Can you be quiet, kitty?"

I couldn't stop my gasp. "Kitty?"

"You're warm and soft in my hand."

I curled my fingers into the material of the tablecloth. "You have a dirty mouth?"

"Not usually." He pressed a kiss under my ear and worked my clit with his thumb. I couldn't ride his fingers, or it'd be obvious what he was doing, but he pumped them in and out of me at a perfect pace.

I'd been getting myself off all week. It should take longer than this, but energy was coiling tight and quick. An explosion was imminent.

Was I a secret voyeur?

No, I liked my privacy. Was it the thrill of getting caught? Maybe, but I suspected it was the man and the way he murmured in my ear, sending shivers racing down my spine to coalesce with the firestorm raging between my legs.

"You like having me inside you, don't you? I fucking knew it, but I never thought you'd be this wet for me. Wait until I bury my face in that heat—"

"God, Vaughn," I groaned, barely holding my volume down. Every muscle tensed to keep from shouting and convulsing next to him. I needed to come, not get 911 called on me.

"Take it, kitty—and let go."

Each of my fists was full of tablecloth. I ground my teeth together as the strongest detonation went off inside me. I should get a fucking Oscar from the way I kept my composure.

"Vaughn," I whined.

"I feel you coming. Your greedy body is clamping around my fingers. So fucking tight."

My shudders slowly subsided and he removed his hand to rest on my thigh. "I bet you're more delicious than any dessert this fucking town serves."

~

Vaughn

The elevator doors closed behind us. I crowded her against the wall. I didn't care if we had a straight shot to our floor or had to stop every five seconds to pick up people, I was tasting her.

I claimed her mouth. Her fingers dug into my coat. We continued going up, but it wasn't fucking quick enough. Finally, we stopped, and I made myself pull out of the hot depths of her mouth. I wanted to be inside this female in every way.

When the doors opened, we were positioned much like when we'd left the restaurant. Her in front of me so I could hide the wet spot on the back of her dress and she could conceal the raging boner I was sporting.

We walked to our room like that, and it was like a

special dance step. Quick, quick, turn. Quick, quick, there was our door.

When we got into the room, she yanked me inside and pressed me up against the wall. Her body was draped against me. "How did you do that? How did you make me come so fast?"

A slow grin spread across my face. She wasn't upset; she was honestly shocked at her body's reaction to me. Maybe I should be surprised too. I'd never been this turned on in my life.

I gripped her hips and spun us until her back was against the wall. "Don't you know, kitty? We're mates."

The pupils of her eyes were large, and this was the only time I'd allow the vibrancy of her irises to be dimmed. I tugged open the sleeveless side of her dress. Her tit was there, ripe and ready. No bra. "Christ, Memphis. You're going to give me an aneurysm. You went out in nothing but the dress and heels?"

"Is that bad?" she asked, her voice husky.

"It's the fucking best." I took her nipple into my mouth. She arched into me, and as much as I wanted to spend time on her breasts, I'd have to wait.

I needed her to come against my face. A guy had to be put out of his misery eventually.

Dropping to my knees, I lifted a swath of her skirt and ducked under. She hitched a leg smoothly to my shoulder, and I loved her lack of insecurity. She researched airports and fine dining. Her nerves didn't stop her. With sex, she was all in. No hesitation, and god, what an aphrodisiac.

I licked through her seam and attacked her clit like I had ten seconds to get her off or the world was going to blow. She buried her hands in my hair and rode my face the way I knew she wanted to ride my fingers earlier.

"Vaughn." Her moan was loud too. We were going to earn some complaint calls tonight.

Needing back inside her, I thrust two fingers into her warm channel. She was still wet and waiting for me.

Her hands tightened around the strands of my hair. She could pull them all out, and I wouldn't stop unless she told me to.

Licking and sucking, I knew she was ready to explode when her greedy body locked onto my fingers.

"I can't believe it," she panted. "I'm coming again already."

Fuck yeah, she was.

And she did. My name echoed through the room, and she pumped her hips against me. I lapped up as much as I could. I couldn't get enough.

So I'd try for more. Shifters were enhanced in so many ways. How many times could a shifter come in one night?

How many times could I come? Just in case, I was giving her another orgasm.

She was there for it. "Yes."

I didn't let up. My fingers, my tongue—I stroked her off a third time.

When that one was done, she drew my head away, gazing down at me from her lofty height. I was like a servant at her feet, and I didn't mind. Just like she didn't mind taking orders from me. It had to be a relief for her, after everything. I could provide that.

"How many times are we doing this?" she asked, breathless.

"How many do you want?"

Pink crested her cheeks, and her lips parted like she was still panting. "I want you inside me. Get undressed."

"Yes, ma'am."

Her lips twitched. I rose, but she put her hands on my chest. "Wait. Let me."

She stripped me down. One article of clothing at a time. First, the coat. She meticulously hung it up.

"That shouldn't be so sexy," I said in a rough voice. She did the same with my shirt. With my pants, she folded them so the crease would stay crisp and hung them up.

Then she kneeled. My boxers were doing a poor job at containing my obnoxious erection, but she bypassed those and took each sock off, then folded them together and tossed them toward my suitcase.

I was ready to burst. I'd never experienced this level of meticulous foreplay—and that was what it was. She was ramping me up, and I couldn't get enough. I almost wanted more clothes for her to take off.

The primitive part of my brain liked her kneeling in front of me.

She hooked her fingers around the waistband of my boxers. I held my breath as she inched them over my cock and pulled down.

My erection bobbed in front of her face, so sensitive I could feel her warm breath caress the length. She caught my gaze as she folded my underwear, taking her time.

"You're a fucking tease, kitty."

"Now that's something I've never been accused of." She tossed the clothing toward my suitcase. Neither of us cared where it landed.

I thought she'd rise, and I'd haul her toward the bed,

but she gripped the base of my cock. My entire body jolted. "Fuck."

Her saucy mouth tilted into a grin, and she parted her lips and leaned forward.

My focus was only on her. Her red lips wrapped around the tip of my dick and she licked across the crown.

I groaned, long and hard. Nothing I'd done for myself could compare. The heat of her lips and the sight of her before me almost ended the night. I could blow and pass out from euphoria, but she sucked me farther into her mouth. I was too far from a wall to hold on to it, so I stuffed my hand into her hair, but I was gentle. This female deserved the best, and it wasn't me yanking her head around.

She bobbed along my cock, her hand working the base, and I had to stagger back.

"If you even look at me, I'm going to blow," I wheezed. I had to be inside her, and I was only human. I could fuck her more than once tonight, but I needed some recovery. I drew her to her feet, and she licked across one of my nipples as she went. "You're naughty."

Her throaty laugh made my dick twitch.

"Raise your arms." She did as I asked. I lifted her dress over her head. "Want me to hang this up?"

"If you take the time, I'm going to shred it."

Chuckling, I lifted her against me. The exquisite pain of her body squeezing my erection between us was almost enough to get me off, but I held it together.

I reached the bed. "Tell me, Memphis. Be honest. Do I need to devour you again before I'm inside you?"

emphis

THE MAN TOWERING OVER ME, looking at me like I was a smorgasbord made just for him, was really asking if I needed to come again.

I could orgasm once more, but I was desperate to have him fill me. His fingers were more than I could've imagined, but that magnificent cock jutting toward me wasn't something I wanted to waste time around.

I planted my heels in the bed, dropping my knees wide open. "Get inside me, Vaughn."

"Kitty, your wish is my command."

The weird thing was, I thought he meant it. His words weren't sexy banter. He'd been looking after me all day. Since he gave me my birthday present on the plane. I'd never gotten presents from nonfamily members.

He prowled over to me, hooked one of my legs over

his shoulder, and planted himself at my entrance. The broad tip of him pressed inside me, filling me in a way I'd never felt before. I was complete, like I'd found my match. My breath caught and his expression turned worried.

No, no slowing down. I dug my other heel into his ass cheek. "Fuck me, Vaughn."

He powered all the way in. I cried out, and he groaned and stalled, letting us both get used to being connected.

"Fuck, Memphis. I never thought...I never thought it could be this good."

"So good."

He pulled almost all the way out and surged back in. From there, I held on for dear life. He fucked me like the orgasm led to a jackpot.

I tumbled over another peak, arching off the mattress, one hand twisted in the covers and the other hanging on to him. He was hitting exactly the right places and the dusting of hair trailing down his abs was just the light sensation my clit needed.

"Vaughn," I moaned.

"Scream my fucking name, kitty." He pounded into me.

"Vaughn!"

He thrust once, twice, and then he exploded. My waning climax kicked back up. His hot release filled me and my ecstasy notched higher. I'd heard sex was better between mates, but now I was a believer.

He collapsed on top of me, then reared back. "Shit, am I heavy? Nah, you're fucking strong."

A breathy laugh left me. We were still connected, but I was in no hurry to move. Especially not when he nuzzled his nose into my neck and inhaled. He brushed a hand down my side and left it resting on my hip.

After a few moments, he lifted his head. "Shifters aren't like sex gods, are they? Like...they can go again and again and again? I'm too close to forty to do that, but I can make it good for you."

I squeezed my hands through his hair. I'd been dying to mess it up since we'd met. "You already made it good."

"That's your way of saying yes." He pulled out and scooted down my body until he could suck a nipple into his mouth.

Desire I thought was sated flared again. "I'm saying I'm very satisfied."

He rolled his tongue around my peak and it was like an electrical cord was connected to my sensitive clit. "And I'm hearing you can come again."

He continued to crawl down until he was between my thighs and my knees were hooked over his shoulders. The sight of him like that was almost enough to get me off again. "You don't have to—"

He lightly licked across my swollen nub and I was lost. Vaughn could do whatever the hell he wanted to my body.

～

VAUGHN

MY CLINICAL BRAIN had convinced me that my sex drive would naturally wane. That I wouldn't be able to have multiple orgasms in one night anymore. My reality was proving it wrong.

I turned Memphis to face the window. She had on a robe with the tie hanging free at her side. The front gaped open, and she was reflected in the glass. I had on my own robe, loosely tied and was behind her. She wiggled her hips into me. I tapped her ass cheek. "Soon."

"I want you in me again."

I'd been in her twice. She'd gotten off countless times. I might be doing more sexually than I thought I was capable of at this age, but I had to pace myself, which somehow only heightened the experience. I wasn't a teen trying to have sex without getting caught. But as much as I looked forward to feeling her body pulse and clamp around my cock, I also couldn't wait to sleep with her in my arms. A sated, sleepy Memphis shared the pinnacle of my fantasy—along with the Memphis who couldn't get enough of me.

We'd played around in the hot tub. She rode my hand while I tongued her breasts. I had plans to do that again —several times—before we checked out.

I slipped the robe down her arms and tossed it onto a chair. Then I plastered her hands against the cool glass of the window.

Keeping my hands over hers, I whispered in her ear, "Keep them there."

She didn't balk. The thought that someone might see us didn't bother her. She'd been worried in the restaurant and I wanted to keep what was between us private too, but the thrill was there. I liked seeing the red, yellow, blue, and green lights bouncing off her soft skin.

I'd been over every inch of her body.

No wonder I'd been miserable for months. I'd been missing this fine piece of female under the same roof. A female who hadn't pouted or begged for my attention. A female who'd let me be my pissy self while she dealt with shit like a boss.

I was falling for my mate.

I laid a kiss on top of her shoulder and met her gaze in the glass. Her eyes were so fucking vibrant and the physician in me was delighted over the fact that her eye color was so damn unique. That she was outside the realm of medical experience. She was outside my job and maybe I'd needed that.

Running my hands up and down her body, I held her gaze. Then I stroked around to her abdomen and down her belly. "I'm going to watch you come."

"You've been watching me come all night." Her breath puffed against the window.

"It's morning now." I rubbed her sex with my palm and her eyes went hooded.

"I like how responsive you are."

"It's you. Us."

"Because we're mates?" I thrust a finger inside her and continued small circles with my palm.

"Yes," she said, need in her voice.

"I never knew it could be like this." My cock was poking out of the robe. I could shove inside her, but I wanted her closer to the edge. "Your hot little pussy is greedy for me, kitty."

She whimpered and ground into my hand. I had to put my forehead on her shoulder to collect myself, or I'd paint her ass with my release.

"You have a dirty mouth, doctor," she murmured.

"Only with you," I breathed against her ear, loving the shivers racking her body. "Only with you."

I'd been, for lack of a better description, clinical before.

"Say it again." She undulated her hips, and she was pulsating around my fingers, already close.

I untied my robe and let the flaps fall wide. Sliding inside her, I growled into her ear, "This greedy pussy is all mine."

"Yours."

My fingertips only rested on her clit and I lazily thrust in and out. I might've looked relaxed, but I was standing on a ledge, waiting to plummet. I wasn't going without her.

I pulled out and slammed into her. "Mine."

"Yours." Her hands were flat against the glass, but her fingers curled. "Oh, god, yours."

She was coming. I held her stare in the window and chanted, "Mine, mine, mine."

I kept the pressure on her clit and dug my other hand into her hip, tipping her out so I could bury myself deeper. Then I exploded with her. The strength of the orgasm should've made my knees buckle as I rocketed into her in short bursts, pulsing hot jets into her needy body.

She sagged against the window, her cheek and tits pressed to the glass. If someone saw us, they were getting a hell of a view.

I pulled out of her and took my robe off. When she turned, I draped it around her and led her to the bed. She tossed the robe on the same chair the other one was draped over and got under the covers.

In the bathroom, I grabbed a towel, and on my way back to the bed, I got a water from the mini-fridge. I handed both to her.

"Are you always this thoughtful?" she joked, but I realized that she didn't know.

"Yes. I promise you'll see it from now on."

Her expression turned to stone. "You know about promises with our kind."

That breaking them could be a death sentence if the one let down wanted to pursue the issue? Yes. "Won't be a problem."

I crawled in beside her and drew her into me. Tracing my fingers over her side and hip, I waited for sleep to claim me, but I had to make sure she was comfortable enough to sleep first.

She was quiet but awake.

"Penny for your thoughts," I said.

"I think a doctor could afford more." She snuggled into me. "Besides, I'm a dragon. I like gems."

"I can dig a pearl out of an oyster. They might still sell them on the Strip like they did when Cricket and I were kids."

"No need to kill an oyster." She chuckled and fell quiet again.

I stared at the wall, wondering if this weekend was too little too late or if I had time to work on her trust. I'd made her wait months for me to be decent. I had to be ready to work months to get to her heart.

"I was wondering how this would change things when we returned," she said quietly. "Nothing will be different as far as shifters go. The only change is that we're having sex."

I was tempted to joke that I might not be such a moody bastard if I was getting laid regularly, but her concern was a valid one. "I'm working hard to understand." That wasn't right. I did understand. I hated that it was a reality in her world—and that world was now mine. "I'll keep trying, Memphis. I promise."

"Don't. I know you mean to keep your promise, but it's stressful for me."

The staggering realization dawned on me. "You'd have to carry out the punishment."

Her silky hair rubbed along my arm as she nodded.

"I don't want to make your life harder."

"I didn't want to do that to you either." But she wouldn't be able to help it.

"I'm here, Memphis. We've been through a lot already—more than a lot of shifter couples, I'd guess—and I'm still here. We'll work through whatever comes up."

The tension slowly left her body until her breathing was even. I continued to stare at the wall long after she fell asleep. Promise or not, I was a man of my word.

Vaughn

"THOSE ASSHOLES." Memphis was looking at the itinerary.

I peered over her shoulder. "Dining in the dark? What's wrong with that?"

Her lips were quirked when she looked at me. "I'm not the one who'll have a problem seeing in the dark."

I chuckled. It was a tongue-in-cheek event on the itinerary. Today, we'd wandered up and down the Strip in a way I hadn't done since, well, since Cricket woke up married to Maverick, but not since my parents were alive.

She folded the paper and shoved it into the pocket of her frayed jeans. She was wearing athletic shoes and a light sweater with horizontal blocks of color. She looked tough but youthful. "We can skip it. You want to go to your old job anyway."

"No, I don't." The look she gave called me on my bull-shit. "Have I mentioned it that much?"

"A few times."

Those times flooded back to me. *My old hospital is right over there.*

Six months ago, I'd only be halfway done with my day.

At my old hospital…

"More than a few times," I said, and she smirked.

"You mind? Maybe I need some closure. My departure was rather abrupt."

"It's fine. I've never been in a hospital."

"You don't know how fortunate you are."

We walked back to the parking garage our rental car was parked in. She took in all the sights and our silence was comfortable, not the tension-filled air from Peridot Falls. As I pulled out into Vegas traffic, I let my mind wander to Memphis's questions when we were in bed. What would things be like when we returned home?

I thought of Memphis's house as home, but now that I was back in Vegas, it had a different ring. The nostalgia might be fucking with me. Part of me still didn't feel like I belonged in Peridot Falls, but Las Vegas was no longer my home.

At my old workplace, I pulled into a parking spot after nearly turning into the employee parking lot. If Memphis noticed, she didn't point it out.

We got out, and she glanced down at herself. "I'm going to look like a patient, aren't I?"

I was dressed similarly to how I would've dressed before. I didn't take to scrubs, preferring to stand out to my patients, to be someone the kids didn't identify as hospital other than my lab coat. Other pediatricians wore fun scrubs, but I didn't have a zany personality, and I didn't care to make false promises. "People might think you're a visitor too."

She smirked, and I led her inside. Just like walking the Strip, Memphis was quiet, soaking in the sights and sounds. Finally, she said, "There're more people on one floor than in Peridot Falls."

"Maybe two or three floors." I put my hand on her back just as we turned toward a bank of elevators.

They dinged open and an elderly couple and a lone guy filed out. Behind them was a pretty, petite blonde with big doe eyes.

"Vaughn." Her grin was wide, her teeth immaculately white. "Ohmigod, you're back. Get tired of the country?"

"Bethany, hi. No, just back showing..." Shit. I didn't tell my coworkers exactly why I'd up and moved. Just that Cricket moved, and I couldn't be across the country from her and maybe it was time for a change. "...my wife around."

Bethany's eyes grew comically large, but the situation wasn't funny. Hurt rolled off Memphis as she stood stiffly next to me. Bethany's gaze dropped down to Memphis, taking in her casual outfit. The girl wasn't catty, but her shock was understandable.

"Wife. Hi." Her astonishment rang through the area.

"Memphis, this is Bethany. We used to, uh, work together." We used to do more together, but the fact scrolled through my head like an announcement at the bottom of a new show. After last night, after the last few months, I didn't remember the specifics of other women, only that I'd been with them. But I had been mated to Memphis when I came to Vegas to quit my job. Did she feel like a dirty little secret?

"Memphis?" Bethany stuck her slender hand out. "What a neat name."

Memphis gave her hand a squeeze. "Nice to meet you." She was civil, but her voice echoed emptily.

Bethany playfully punched my shoulder. "You move fast. The fresh air must've done you good."

My laugh was wooden. Memphis's brow inched up.

"Well." Bethany brandished her travel-size coffee mug. "I need a refill. Curt's up there. He'd love it if you stopped by. Um...congrats, you two."

She scurried away, and I sighed, staring at the silver elevator. We'd missed the empty one and were back to waiting.

How did I explain? "That was, uh..."

"A coworker you used to fuck?"

I was grateful for her shifter instinct. "I was going to say awkward, but you're right too."

"Is this Curt going to be just as shocked about your wife?"

I should've stayed far away from this place. This hospital was my past, and being here was a sign I wasn't moving on as I should. It was Memphis's birthday trip, for fuck's sake. "Yes. He's going to be shocked. I said I was moving because Cricket was, and they all know how close I am to her."

"Mm."

The door dinged open and after it was empty, we entered.

I punched the button for my old floor. "When I quit, my head was still spinning, and I was so angry."

She crossed to me, put her hands on either side of my face, and planted a kiss on my lips. "I get it. But I'm kind of enjoying how uncomfortable you are."

"Revenge?" My pride in how Memphis handled everything soared.

"Something like that."

On my old floor, nurses and aides bustled by. When we reached my old mentor's office, the door was closed.

"He's busy." I put a hand on the small of her back, liking how she absolutely didn't need me to guide her but that she didn't mind the hint of possessiveness I couldn't escape. "We can go."

"Why? Did you sleep with Curt too?"

I chuckled. "He's married with grown kids, but I've heard people call him a hottie."

The door opened, and a little boy with his parents came out. The boy's face brightened. "Dr. V!"

I squatted down. "Nelson, my guy."

He flew into me for a hug. "I thought you quit."

I glanced up at my mentor, watching us from the doorway, his curious gaze going from me to Memphis. "I came back for a visit, and you're the cherry on top."

Nelson ignored my reply and gazed up at Memphis. "Who's she?" His frank question was blatant in only the way kids could be, but his expression was neutral, maybe a little intrigued.

"This is my wife."

"She why you left?"

"Yes." I stayed crouching down. Nelson was eight, but because of his illness, he was on the shorter side.

"You guys have kids yet?"

I laughed, a less wooden sound than with Bethany. "No, not yet."

"How many you gonna have?"

Nelson's mom tucked Nelson into her side. "We need to let Dr. V. go." She grinned at me. "But I'd like to give you a hug. Without you and Dr. Curt, we wouldn't have gotten the good news."

Nelson had been getting treated for a rare form of cancer, and from her smile, the good news must mean he was in remission. I gave Nelson's mom a hug and shook his dad's hand.

When they were gone, I introduced Memphis to Curt. Keeping the chat to a few minutes out of respect for Curt's time—and Memphis's, I wrapped it up, got a hearty handshake, back pat, and then we were back at the elevator.

Memphis scanned around her. Her silence had an edge.

"We shouldn't have come," I said. "This week is your time."

"We're a couple," she said evenly.

"Then what's wrong?" I dropped my voice so only she could hear.

The elevator dinged open, but for the ride down, we weren't the only ones on it. I waited until we were closed into the car. I didn't have to prod. Her contemplative gaze was aimed out the windshield. The muscle in her jaw pulsed lightly.

"Kids—when and how many?" She pinned me with her direct stare. "We didn't use protection last night."

We didn't, and it'd been natural. How didn't I think of the repercussions? Did I want a kid nine months from now? I knew her people expected us to procreate, but that didn't mean I'd bring a kid into a relationship that wasn't stable.

I was a doctor—this shouldn't have taken me off guard. Yet, I'd been around long enough to know that sometimes our education and knowledge made us complacent. We were just as guilty of thinking it couldn't happen to us.

Had I been complacent?

No. I'd been with someone I couldn't wait one more second to be with. I didn't have any condoms on me, and I doubted she did either.

Then why was my pulse picking up with a rising tide of panic in my stomach?

A faint sense of hurt emanated from her frown. "Memphis."

She shook her head. "We can talk about this later, but maybe pick up some condoms if you don't want to have a kid right now."

"That's not what I'm saying."

"We should be clear. I told you what the council expects, but this is about what we want. Do you want to have kids with me?"

A yes should've spilled out right away, but no words gathered on my tongue.

MEMPHIS

WE GOT BACK to the hotel. There'd be no dining in the dark. After such a good day, today had ended on a downer. The roller coaster of this weekend was brutal. The mate who you thought hated you, but who couldn't get enough of you, and your chemistry was off the charts, but who was really just good for the sex. He ultimately didn't want you to be the mother of his children.

A year ago, I wouldn't have said I was maternal. Six

months ago, I wouldn't have said it. Having a kid was my duty, and I didn't think of it beyond that. I wanted a mate first. A real family, like the one I'd grown up in.

My hopes weren't raised for long, but they were crushed hard.

"Are we going to talk about this?" Vaughn unbuttoned the sleeve of his dress shirt and rolled a cuff up. Sexy as sin.

My body lit like a neon sign, but mentally, I wasn't there. "Your reaction spoke loud enough."

"Come on, Memphis. You've granted me a lot of leeway while I adjusted—I need a little more."

I spun away from the window. My handprints were still on the glass from our first night here. "What about me? Everything has been about you. *You* were forced to be with me, not that I saved your life, so I didn't have to kill you. So I didn't have to kill you and tarnish my relationship with my brother and his mate." I ran a hand through my hair. I should buzz it again. "What about me when I have to live in my house like I'm an unwanted impostor? What about me when I have to walk around the place I grew up in and everyone knows my mate hates me? What about me that no one—not even my mate—thinks I'm suitable maternal material? *Fuck*." I turned back to the window.

He took a couple of steps toward me.

"Don't."

He stopped. "Memphis. We have to talk. It's not cut and dry. Does the thought that you could find you're pregnant in a couple of weeks fuck with my head? Yes. So does the idea that any kids I father with you will be able to change into dragons. Motherfucking dragons, Memphis." He paced, and I followed his path in the window. "I can what? Teach them baseball? My kids will be able to fly. And breathe fire. And heal. I'm a doctor, and I can't heal. I can only practice medicine and hope to hell some of it works."

I bit the inside of my cheek. During my "what about me" pity party, I hadn't thought of his concerns other than not wanting kids with me.

He stopped. "And then they grow up and our oldest will have to kill people?"

I squeezed my eyes shut. Our oldest child would be the next ruler of the clan. It was a fact I didn't put much thought into. "Yes."

"How do I raise a kid to become a killer?"

I glanced over my shoulder. "Is that what you think of me?"

"No. But you have to kill. What did your parents do?"

Sighing, I turned all the way around. "We don't know any different. Don't you see, Vaughn? There aren't these questions. It just is. I don't sit around and ponder it."

"Well, I do."

I lifted my hands. "So, we wait."

"And if I'm not willing to bring kids into a hostile world?"

The backs of my eyes burned, matching the sting in my chest. "Then Maverick and Cricket's oldest will take my place if I don't have kids."

He scoffed. "Cricket can't raise a killer."

"Will you quit calling me a killer?"

He threw his arms out. "It's not an observation I can get over."

"I need to shower." I couldn't tell him the stink of the hospital lingered on me. The smell of sickness and anti-septic and the strength of the emotions in the place were making me nauseous. He'd probably panic and think I was experiencing the quickest-ever morning sickness.

"Memphis," he said as I walked past him.

"We've said everything we had to say. Talking any more about this will hurt both of us more."

I disappeared into the bathroom, locking the door behind me.

CHAPTER
ELEVEN

Vaughn

LANDING BACK in Minneapolis wasn't the disappointment it should've been. It should've been the end of a week we wanted to keep going. A bittersweet happening—glad to be home, wishing we could still be on vacation.

I was glad the trip was over, but the trees around Peridot Falls loomed on the horizon and anxiety clawed at my gut.

The silence that filled the day after our fight had been the worst. An almost complete setback. We'd slept in the same bed, but she took a long bath in the bathroom with the door locked. In first class on the flight home, she read one of the books she'd downloaded instead of one of the ones I'd given her. Those she'd read in the hotel room while we were sitting around. Instead of sex, she used the books to create a wall between us.

I guess I'd done that all by myself.

Since we'd driven to the airport separately, I had let her have a head start. It was her house, and she deserved to settle in and unpack while I wasn't there. Besides, I had to figure out how unreasonable I was being.

I drove into Peridot Falls and went to Cricket's place. She met me at the door, her expression solemn.

"What'd you hear?"

"Nothing other than Maverick said Memphis was strangely distant when she called to tell us she was back." Cricket tilted her head. "She said the vacation was *fine*."

For fuck's sake. A cold wind snaked across my neck like a little bitch slap. Cricket stepped back. "You might as well come in. Maverick went to talk to Levi. I'm sure he and Maverick are plotting how to get it out of her what happened."

I stepped in.

She shut the door harder than expected. "I know all this is my fault because I ran off with Maverick, and I'm really trying to give you the benefit of the doubt, but dammit, Vaughn. I want you to be happy and you seem to be doing everything you can to prevent that."

Irritated—at myself, at my sister, at the world—I started pacing, hoping I didn't track dirt into her house, but also not caring. "Is it so crazy to question having kids just to put them in a position to kill others?"

Her mouth snapped shut.

I continued my path back and forth. "The week was awesome. We connected, and then I made an idiot decision to visit the hospital."

"Why?"

Cricket sounded so clueless my frustration grew. "Because it was my second home. I spent more time there than I did in my own bed. Those people weren't just my colleagues, they were my lifelines. My social hour. The patients were every goal I wanted to attain in my life. I had a purpose there, Cricket. The only thing that would come close here is fatherhood. I've seen what she's had to do. *You've* seen what she's had to do. How do you raise a kid to do that, Bug?"

"You won't be alone," she said softly. "This town will become your hospital. Memphis will teach them about being a ruler. She and her brothers will teach them about being dragon shifters. The neighbors will help teach your children how to be part of a clan. And you'll teach them how to be a good person. How to care about others and how best to use their healing. They'll have their own goals that won't be related to being a dragon shifter."

I stopped. When had my sister gotten so damn insightful and smart? If I'd seen how well she read the world around her, perhaps I wouldn't have rushed to Peridot Falls thinking she'd made the worst, most dangerous decision of her life.

The front door opened and Maverick pushed inside. "Is that what all this is about? Kids?"

Goddamn shifter hearing. I didn't want my insecurities spread around the family, but if they could help me, then maybe it was for the best.

"Because Memphis gets enough snide comments from the council about her maternal fitness."

"Are they still saying that?" My rage swept through me so hot I thought I should go back outside.

Maverick arched a brow, anger and sarcasm gleaning in his bright eyes. "Most everyone who comments on Memphis and kids in the same breath has been saying that since you two mated."

"It's not her maternal instinct I'm worried about. It's my paternal one. I'm more worried about raising kids to take Memphis's place. She'll do just fine as a mother." I didn't know how I knew that. Before the vacation, I might've wondered. Being away from here, from all the changes and questions of my future, had made it easier to see her contemplative nature. She wasn't cold or aloof; she was thinking and studying. She wasn't calculating or reactive; she was forming the best judgment-based decision possible, and putting up with others' bullshit wasn't part of the benefits package in her job.

Any questions she had about motherhood, she'd look up. She'd research just as she had airports and first class and fine dining.

"She's my sister, and I was honestly a little worried." Maverick shrugged. "I love her, but she's never been warm and fuzzy."

"Did you give her a safe area to be that way?" I snapped. Memphis was full of blistering heat and passion. I'd been her space to be that way for a few moments.

Cricket stepped into Maverick's side. "If it's not having her as a mother to your kids, then what is it? Is it really the shifters and the violence? Or...is it all about you?"

My first instinct was to scoff. Then...shit. Memphis had asked what about her—and I'd still ignored her. I was making myself the center of the relationship again. Shouldering all the responsibility, just like she would do with any children we might have if I didn't get my head out of my ass. "I've gotta go." I was almost out the door when I turned back. "Thanks for the talk." I gave them a curt nod and rushed out the door.

It took minutes to get to the house. A light was on deep inside where her bedroom was. I left my suitcase in the car once again, as if I needed to be prepared to track her down again, and marched in. I didn't call her name but stalked straight to her bedroom.

The door was cracked open. She was sprawled on her bed, staring at the ceiling, hands hooked across her belly.

I didn't stop and crawled right onto the bed on top of her. She pushed to her elbows, but I planted a kiss on her lips until she dropped back. Then I broke away, staying inches from her. "I'm afraid. Fucking scared of screwing this up. I don't know if you know this, but doctors are arrogant. We're cocksure because we have to be. Too much riding on our decisions. And this thing with the kids...I'm putting myself in the center. I wouldn't do that at work. I'd call in help. Ask colleagues."

She framed my face with her hands, gazing into my eyes for several moments. "You're going to ask friends to raise our kids?" There was a slight tease to her tone that gave me hope.

"I have you. Just like when you came back from that hunt and I sat with you, you'll be there with me. I want kids, Memphis. Dammit, I'm pretty damn scared to say that too. I thought I'd already be married and have a family, and a big part of me had given up on the idea."

Incredible vulnerability traced through her eyes before she clamped her teeth together. Her gaze skittered away. "What if I suck as a mom?"

"Do you suck at anything?"

"There's a reason Levi and Briony don't ask me to help in the bakery."

"If they ever start a line of breakfast burritos, they have to call you. If they don't, I'm not eating them."

She laughed, her body shaking lightly under mine. Her smile died and a long breath left her. "I don't like thinking about my kids having to do what I've done."

"Then we make sure they're not alone. We make sure they have us, and Maverick and Cricket's kids, and Levi and Briony's kids. If we have more than one, we make sure they ask each other for help, that they can approach their cousins or their aunts and uncles."

She stroked her gaze over my face. "Is that what we've done with our siblings?"

"I was a helicopter older brother after our parents died, and I sure as shit never let Cricket in on what was going on in my life."

"Same."

"Guess we gotta work on that." Having her underneath me wasn't lost on my body. The stress of the argument gladly faded to lust. I took one of her hands and put it above her head. I did the same with the other. "Keep them there."

"Are we having make-up sex?"

"I'm making everything up to you, so you're going to lie there and get pleasured."

She laughed and rolled her hips into me, then froze. "What about...protection?"

I pushed the hem of her black hoodie over her breasts. "Pretty hard to have kids when using a condom."

"Are you...are you sure?"

I couldn't blame her for doubting me. I tugged the cups of her bra down. "Let me show you how sure I am. The first time might be kind of quick." I didn't like the insecurity lingering in her eyes. I'd come inside of her a thousand times if that was what it took to let her know I wanted this.

The more I thought about the family I had assumed was getting farther out of my reach, the more excited I got. Memphis with a rounded belly. Hard, flinty gaze outside of the house, warm and molten inside.

I dragged her pants off and kneeled between her feet. She'd taken her boots off. I hadn't undressed, and I wasn't going to take the time. Sleeping next to her and not being able to touch her after days of losing myself inside of her was a special torture I had to reassure my dick I didn't plan to repeat.

"Spread your legs, kitty."

She groaned and did as I ordered. "You get me with that kitty. It's not right. It shouldn't work."

"But it makes you wet as soon as it leaves my mouth."

She bent her knees, giving me a better view. "A lot to do with you makes me wet."

I ripped the zipper strangling my erection down, freeing it, and crawled between her thighs. Her pussy was glistening and ready for me. I didn't wait. Her need matched mine.

Shoving inside her, I nearly lost my hold on the mattress and collapsed on top of her. Somehow, I kept myself braced on my hands.

She hooked her ankles behind my ass. "I love how you fill me."

I pounded into her. The sound of our bodies slapping filled the room, along with our dueling groans.

I didn't have to play with her clit. She was nearing her explosion, and I lowered myself to my elbows. "I'm going to come inside you. Because I want you and I want this."

She lost control. Her body constricted around me, and we both tumbled over the steep edge. She milked everything I had, and I gave it to her. We'd been doing this all weekend, but this time was different. We weren't lost on new lust. Old concerns weren't stuffed in the corner trying to get out. Fears weren't surpassed.

For once, we were real with each other, and we were together. And that was the way it was supposed to be. I knew that now.

~

Memphis

I was living a dream. I woke up—in Vaughn's arms. I went to work, and sometimes I met him for lunch, or he brought food to my office. Then I went home, and we cooked together. We ate together. He talked about his workday, and I discussed mine.

Two weeks of domestic bliss and I thought I was addicted.

Another workday was done and we were sitting down to a spaghetti meal we had prepared together.

I pushed my noodles around, almost afraid to ask my next question. "You seem happier with your job."

Surprise flitted across his face. A crease formed as he seriously thought about what I'd said. "Yeah. I am." His smile was lopsided. "I guess that's what happens when it's not my entire life."

"It's easier for me to go to work when you're at home when I'm done."

His grin was sexy and his eyes full of promise. "Speaking of...I'd like to get out more."

"How do you mean?" I stuffed my mouth full of noodles before I peppered him with questions that were so unlike me. *Are you sure you're happy? What happens when the honeymoon period wears off or we have another argument? Do you think you could love me one day?*

We hadn't said the words, and I might be an independent girl and all the bullshit that came with it to protect my heart, but I didn't want to be the first to make a move. I'd made him mate me. The other option was death. I needed him to be the one to say it first.

"I'm sick of the office. It's better since I've been sleeping in the bedroom, but I'm used to moving around a lot." He frowned at a meatball. "I don't heal like you, and I'm going to develop a killer case of sciatica to nurse if I keep sitting in the damn office chair."

"You want to commute to the city?"

I wasn't going to tell him what to do for work more than I had, but I didn't want him to drive so often and so far. A lot of dragon shifters were lost in car accidents. A higher amount than humans because we avoided hospitals. Our blood would test weird and it didn't work to get rolled into an ER on death's door and heal before a surgeon's eyes.

Since we lived in rural areas, around a lot of other shifters, our accidents were often on desolate roads with no witnesses, possibly with injuries more dire than our healing abilities could overcome.

He saved my anxiety by shaking his head. "Is there an open office in city hall? I have a healthy savings built up, and Maverick and Levi have talked about the growth of Peridot Falls. I could build my own space—or lease some property they build. The interior of the space for the cabin rental will be done soon."

I finished chewing. My relief and growing delight weren't only from his denial that he wanted to work in the city. He wanted to make a permanent space outside the home. Did he realize he was thinking of a way to be a permanent part of the town? Of the clan? He already was, but this time it was willingly.

It meant a lot. "Of course. Whatever works best for you, the city would love to help make it happen."

"I'd like space to treat shifters."

"Shifters? Like Josh?" We hadn't learned anything new with Josh or his parents.

He nodded. "Exactly. I could make it more accessible. Less of a...stigma. I could have other information in the office so they are different to come in. There's gotta be some sort of clinical need in the shifter communities."

I rolled more spaghetti onto my fork, took a bite, and thought. "Actually, yes. Silver Lake has a midwife. Giving birth in hospitals isn't allowed, but we still need help. If we're a growing community, there are going to be more births. I'd like to recruit a midwife."

His smile was triumphant. "It'd be like a real clinical office."

I lifted a shoulder as I speared a meatball. "You'd be in charge. Of everything."

He paused, his fork hovering over his plate. "All of it?"

"I don't know shit about medicine. No one here does."

Stunned, he sat back, his hand lax on the table, still holding his utensil. "My own place."

"All yours."

"I...like the sound of that." His laughter rang through the dining room. "I briefly entertained the idea of opening my own practice in Vegas, but the competition would've been fierce. I wanted to practice medicine, not become a marketing guru. Having my own clinic is something I never thought was truly possible."

"It is. If you're going to need space, we have that. You can work out of city hall until a new place is built. Maverick can help you with permits and all that human bureaucratic bullshit."

He pushed his plate away and dropped to his knees to prowl toward me. "You're making my dreams come true, one by one, Memphis."

His gaze flickered enough to catch my attention. I stroked my fingers down his cheek. "Something still bothers you."

"I'm a human among shifters. I want to make sure I'm contributing to the lives of everyone here, but I imagine even Josh could out-bench-press me."

I'd rather he talked to me about his insecurities than hole up in the office and not talk to me for months. Just like I'd rather have him hold me on a bad day rather than cry in the tub all alone. But it was still hard for him, and there was nothing I could do. He needed to accept his humanity the way the rest of us did. Cricket didn't share the same concerns. She'd integrated herself into our society, but he was used to being an alpha male in the human world. The power of the MD behind his name.

For a man who was used to being the big cock in the hospital, a desired specimen to a lot of women, what he thought made him virile in the human world was below average here.

"You're still thinking in terms of brute strength, Vaughn. If that were the case, I wouldn't be ruler. There's always someone who can fight better than me. It's not just cunning either. We prize strength of character, of honor, of the willingness to do what's right and protect others."

"I want to protect you."

I framed his face with my hands. "You do."

His fingers trailed down the long-sleeved shirt I'd worn to work. "I want to be able to protect our children."

All that fucking in Vegas hadn't gotten me pregnant. We weren't trying clock ovulation cycles and best techniques, but we weren't preventing the chance either. In the meantime, we were concentrating on us. Just like tonight.

"You will protect them in so many ways."

"They'll be destined to run this town. They could be targets with me as their dad."

"They could be targets because I'm their mother. We aren't alone. We're a team." I poked the center of my chest. "Just leave any dragons to me."

"Prom—"

I put my finger on his lips. "What'd I say about promises?"

He was starting to lift my top. This wouldn't be the first time we'd finished our dinner cold. "Hmm...you'll have to remind me. Remember to be loud about it."

VAUGHN

MAVERICK and I bent over a layout of the town. He tapped his finger on an area two lots away from the bakery. "The city owns property here." He tapped on the opposite side of town. "And here. Levi and I have been talking about building a commercial building that could be retail or offices. We're in need of both, but you're already here and willing to pay a lease. Offices it is."

"Will the contractors come from within Peridot Falls?"

He nodded. "It's safer that way and better for the local economy." He tapped his fingers on the tabletop. "Josh's dad is actually one of the mechanics. He runs the gas station that supplies the fuel for the contractors' equipment."

"The guy we think might be abusing his son?"

His mouth pressed flat. "We've been spying on him, on his house—nothing. No arguing more than 'Gordy, you forgot to take out the garbage.'"

"That's good." While I was happy to hear the report, a dark cloud descended over my clinic plans. Was it really that forbidden to seek comfort while healing from injuries? I wanted to be a safe space, a useful place. But if seeking human doctors was seen as a weakness, was there a point?

The thought only reinforced my anxiety about becoming a shifter father. They don't teach parenting in medical school, but even shifter parents don't have parenting classes.

"I'm not saying we don't still need services for those in abusive situations," Maverick said like he read my thoughts. He'd probably sensed my change in mood. "Just that Josh's family might not need it."

"Fair. But it won't do any good if no one shows."

"Edith and Josh showed up at your door. We're a clever bunch, and we've grown up hiding ourselves. If one of us wants to go to your office and get a bone set so it's not agony for an hour or two, we'll figure it out."

His words eased my anxiety. A year ago, if I had met someone like Memphis, gotten married, and she'd gotten pregnant right away, I would've been ecstatic. But also petrified. I was a pediatrician. I knew all the horrible things that could happen to kids, be it a bad environment, bad genetics, or bad luck.

I no longer faced a lot of those worries, but they'd been replaced by the unknown.

Maverick drummed his fingertips on the tabletop. "The last few weeks have been good to see, man. You and Memphis."

"They've been good to live. Thanks for getting a second ticket."

"You'll have to thank Levi. I would've left your ass scrambling." He flashed a smile. "Payback."

"I didn't give you that hard of a time," I grumbled good-naturedly. "I didn't have time. You took off with my sister after a few days."

"According to plan." His phone buzzed, and his smile fell. Brow furrowed, he answered. "What's up?"

Whoever was on the other end spoke too low for my human ears to hear. They probably spoke too low for other shifter ears to hear.

Maverick's scowl deepened. "I'll be right there."

Just as he hung up and said, "I've gotta go," my phone rang. It was Memphis.

I answered, "What's wrong?"

"There are some signs of ferals at the Smalls' place. I think they're getting harassed by relatives of the male I terminated."

"Shit, be careful."

"I called Maverick."

"Good." She called him for me. Otherwise, she would've gone alone.

There was a moment's hesitation. "I'll be home when I'm done."

"Be careful." It felt better saying it twice.

"I will. Bye, Vaughn."

Levi swooped through the front door, his dark hair falling over an eye. He gave me a wave and beelined toward the back. A delighted squeal and laughter could be heard from Briony.

I was smiling, much preferring how I wasn't seething with jealousy these days. I gathered the papers just as Levi came back.

"Looks like you and I are in charge of the town for a while," he said.

"How do you mean?"

Levi's expression turned quizzical. "The ruler's mate takes over while the ruler is away from work. Maverick's gone with Memphis. So...you and me."

My mind spun, but I said, "Good thing I cleared my calendar for the meeting."

"I have nothing until you and Maverick decide where to build. Then I'll make it happen."

"Do you help with the feral cases?"

He shook his head. "They just got used to not babying me. I don't anticipate getting called out for terminations anytime soon." The flat set of his lips told me how he felt about that.

"Maybe it's a twin thing."

"It's an overprotective thing. Since our parents died, Memphis holds it all in, shoulders the burden. I'm glad you're there to help carry the load."

I could do that. Just like I could sit with Levi and be generally available while his siblings and my mate faced danger.

CHAPTER
TWELVE

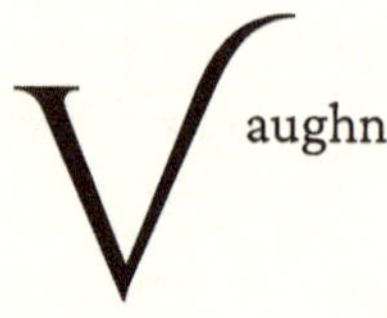aughn

NIGHT HAD FALLEN by the time the bakery closed. Levi and Briony were locking up. I dug my gloves out of my coat pockets. He didn't have more than a sweater—and he was walking. I couldn't blame my humanity for the need for winter wear. My Vegas blood hadn't experienced a winter yet, and it was nothing like going skiing for a weekend at Lake Tahoe.

Anticipation rolled through my veins. I looked forward to my first winter. I anticipated seeing Memphis's cheeks pink from the cold. Warming her up between the sheets. It would be good.

I glanced around the dark town. One dim streetlight shone by city hall, barely meeting any city requirements for adequate lighting on downtown streets. The residents likely preferred it that way.

"What do you think they're up to?" I asked.

Briony had on a sweater but rubbed her hands together and tucked herself into Levi's side. "They might be hunting all night. If it's retaliation, wolf shifters can be cunning as hell. Gran had a hell of a time dealing with them when they got a burr up their ass."

"They should be the ones facing punishment for not taking care of their own," Levi grumbled.

We started walking when tires squealed and a metallic thud echoed from somewhere in the distance.

Briony cocked her head. "That sounded like a big Coke can getting crumpled."

"Car accident." I walked into the middle of the street like it'd help me hear better. "What direction did it come from?"

A long howl pierced the night.

"Fuck." Levi sprinted, ripping his shirt off as he went. He glanced back at Briony. "Stay with him."

She nodded and started nudging me toward city hall. Within two steps, Levi's clothing was spread through the street and he was in his dark dragon form with the bright-green sheen launching into the air. He was bigger than Memphis's dragon, and suddenly, I wanted to see her in her other form. I should've done so earlier.

Now wasn't the time for regrets. Something was wrong.

I extracted myself from Briony's arm, from her surprisingly hard grip. "What's going on? It sounded like an accident."

"Those were shifter wolves."

My pulse sped up, but my doctor brain was kicking in. "Did Memphis and Maverick drive?"

"I doubt it, but I don't know."

"Take me to the accident."

"Vaughn—"

"I'm a doctor, dammit." I started walking toward the main highway. The tire squeal had been faint, but that also meant blacktop of some sort. A ton of dirt roads surrounded Peridot Falls. The location would be easy enough to narrow down. "I can help."

"Not if wolf shifters are trying to fuck with the clan."

"Briony, I don't want to waste time fighting with you. I'm not sitting on the sidelines."

She huffed out a breath and her gaze strayed in the direction where the road through town turned into the highway. "We'll get your car."

In minutes, we were loaded in my car and heading toward the scene. Less than a mile out of town, before the speed limit changed, plastic fragments and glass littered the road. A car was on its side, the trunk plastered against a tree trunk. The vehicle would've taken the tree down, but the car had rolled and spun, losing enough force to be stopped by the thin tree.

I stopped the car with the headlights on the trees. I didn't see any wolves.

Briony opened the door. "Wait here. I'm going to shift before you get out."

I studied the scene. I could hear crying and a faint plea for help. My hands tightened around the wheel. Briony needed to shift fast, or I was going right for the wreckage.

Briony ducked in and shoved her clothing on the seat. Nudity wasn't a concern right now, but I naturally averted my gaze. "Levi's in the trees. I smell wolf shifters, but they're not in the immediate area. If there's any danger, I'll alert you with a growl and you get your ass inside this car."

Only half listening, I got out and rounded the trunk. I had an old medical kit in the trunk that Cricket had given me for Christmas one year. One of the many over the years in the name of keeping the supplies fresh. I kept telling her I was a pediatrician, not an ER doctor, but she claimed I'd never be able to stay away from a medical emergency. She was right.

Hooking the red bag over my shoulder, I jogged toward the car. Broken glass crunched under my feet and I had to dodge plastic bits of the car's frame. Briony padded beside me, having shifted.

I was walking next to a fucking mountain lion.

I circled the car, digging out a flashlight from the jump bag. *Please let the batteries work.*

A faint beam of light marked my path. Carefully making my way through the ditch to the front end, I peered through the windshield.

"C-can you help us?" a female's shaky voice asked.

"I'll do my best." I swept my light over the interior and squinted. She could talk loud enough for me to hear. That was a good start. "My name's Dr. V. How many of you are in the car?"

Leaves rustled next to me, and I jumped when a large form emerged. A dragon. Levi. I didn't dwell on how I could tell he wasn't Maverick. I'd seen a few dragons in Peridot Falls, and they didn't have the peridot-green sheen over their scales.

The replies of the female in the car grew muffled. She was fading. I couldn't even hear her through the shattered windows. Ticks from the engine and dripping fluids could be heard. The stench of burned rubber and gasoline and exhaust attacked my senses.

"I can't hear her." I got closer. The woman was in the passenger seat, bracing herself against the dash to keep from hanging sideways in her seat belt. A man was tipped against the driver's window, his eyes closed, still.

Was there movement in the back seat?

"She said—"

I jumped again. Levi was back in his human form, naked and next to me.

How do they shift that fast? "Fuck—go ahead."

He was undaunted by my jumpiness. "She said it's her and her mate and their three- and five-year-old in the back."

"The child isn't crying anymore." Shit. They were shifters. What did that mean? Was the child healing? Had they sustained injuries beyond their healing capacity? I needed to know. "Can you get the car right side up?"

I was useless if I couldn't get to the patients. I wiped away all concerns about stabilizing the cervical spine and shock and airways. The crash victims needed to be evaluated as soon as possible with whatever means I could provide. There would be no ambulances. No hospitals. The most I could do was make sure they continued breathing and weren't bleeding out.

"Briony." Levi buried his hand in her fur. "Can you help with the car?"

"What's your name?" I called to the passenger.

I didn't hear her respond, but Levi said, "Emily."

"Emily. Steady yourself as much as possible. Levi and Briony are going to make it so I can reach you. Are the kids in the back still buckled in?"

All I caught was an uneven whine and crying.

Briony shifted back and murmured the answer. "She said a door is crumpled into the older kid and a branch came through the window. She thinks they're both seriously hurt. Says their heartbeats are weak."

We had to get moving. "Carefully lower it." I pulled out my phone and made a call. Cricket answered. "Bug, I need you to bring a shitload of towels, a few pillows, and some water bottles to me as fast as possible. Stay in the car with the door locked until you're here." I rattled off directions.

"Got it," she said and hung up.

Relieved and surprised she acquiesced so easily, I stood back and witnessed something I'd have never believed possible. Two people put a car right side up. The creak and groan of metal was concerning, but I kept the word *shifter* on stream through my head. My emergency rotation was a long time ago, and this wasn't ordinary circumstances for what I learned there.

The female cried out again. I ran to the back door and tried to open it. Levi came up next to me, and I stood back. His feet were getting cut up, but he was heedless of the injuries. He yanked the door open.

"What do you need me to do?" Briony asked.

"Check on the driver. Make sure he's breathing. Tell me where he's bleeding and how badly. Emily?" I didn't wait for her to answer. "Since you've been talking to me, I'm going to get the kids out and taken care of. I want you to keep talking to Levi though, so I know how you're doing."

I took her whimper as an answer. There must be words in the sound because Levi let her know everything we were doing.

I peered into the back seat. The kids were in rough

shape. I unbuckled the younger child. A girl. Her cheeks were wet but with tears. I checked her pulse. Thready. Shock, maybe.

The door on the other side was wedged into the boy's side, and the car seat was digging into him. He had a nasty gash on his head like the branch that had punched through the window had knocked him out.

I withdrew with the slight weight of the girl in my arms. "Get him out. Check the same things Briony is and bring him to the back seat of my car."

Grunting through the ditch to the road, I took the girl to my car. I positioned her in the front seat, not caring where she got blood from the myriad of scrapes over her. A nasty laceration was visible through her shirt. I dug out a big gauze pad from my jump bag and pressed it on the laceration, then laid the seat back.

She began to squirm.

"There you go," I said gently. "I'm Dr. V., and I'm going to be taking care of your family."

She started crying.

"Vaughn?"

I straightened. Behind me, a naked Memphis stood in the ditch. I hadn't heard or seen her approach. I was relieved to see her but ecstatic to have more hands. "Can you stay with her while I check on her brother?"

Levi was laying the boy across the back seat.

"Vaughn," Briony called. "I need you over here."

"Keep them breathing and put pressure on any bleeding," I said as I darted away. I was rounding the front of the crashed car when Briony jerked her head toward the passenger.

"I've got the driver," she said. "Check on Emily."

My bag was still slung over my shoulder. The passenger door opened normally, thankfully, but my stomach dropped when my gaze landed on Emily. I couldn't tell if she was a brunette originally or if her hair was too blood-soaked to tell.

Only my experience kept the swear words on my tongue. "Emily, can you hear me?"

Her head lolled, and I caught sight of the two feet of broken tree limb resting on the console. She was bleeding profusely from her shoulder. How the hell.... The branch. She'd been impaled until the car was moved. Emily's situation was dire. I couldn't imagine a shifter recovering from that much blood loss.

"How's the driver?" I asked as I took a pair of scissors from the bag.

As I cut Emily free of the seat belt, Briony filled me in. "The bruise on his head isn't fading yet, and he has a shard of glass in his gut, but his heartbeat is better than Emily's."

I tossed her some gauze. "Normally, we wouldn't remove the glass, but his body will keep trying to heal around it. Take it out and put pressure on it. Keep him in place until we get Emily and the kids taken care of."

Levi was at my side again. "Memphis healed both of the kids. They're sleeping."

A dragon landed on the road behind him. Maverick. He shifted into his human form. Good. I needed another set of hands.

"I can heal a little," Maverick said, coming toward the car, just as careless about where he stepped with his bare feet as his brother. "Who needs me?"

"Everyone but Emily first. I need her laid out so I can

do what I can for any shock." We were already working against so many obstacles.

Between Levi and Maverick, Emily was gingerly laid out on the pavement. Memphis padded across the road. I hated that her feet were getting cut up.

She dropped to a knee with Maverick. "Levi, keep watch for the fucking wolves. I think they're gone, but I wouldn't put it past them to fuck with us right now."

He dipped his head.

Memphis and her twin rested their hands on Emily, Memphis at her head and Maverick at the shoulder.

Maverick was rigid, his concentration on the scalp bleeding. Memphis was on her knees, weaving slightly. I put my hand on her shoulder. "Only enough to keep her from dying."

When she glanced up at me, fatigue lined her face. "It's bad."

Goddammit. I dug through my bag. "Sutures? Will those make her worse or better?"

Maverick shook his head. "Worse. Her body will keep trying to reject the foreign material."

"Can Levi—"

Memphis shook her head and sagged. "Only the ruler. As a twin, Maverick has a little ability." She tapped her brother's hand. "Rest and heal. We'll try again."

I squatted next to her. "Don't risk yourself."

"Like you did coming here?" She was too worn to put much of an edge on her question.

"I had a big cat and a dragon. Don't take the focus away from yourself. Don't hurt yourself."

Her expression was resolute. Just like she'd put herself at risk to terminate shifters, she'd double her efforts to save them.

"I'm going to check on the kids." Otherwise, I would wear her down by pestering her to be careful.

Levi was roaming between the car with the kids to Briony's side and stopping to check on his siblings. At the car, I peeked at the kids. They were sleepy, but their breathing was even and strong, and their pulses were perfect. Two were out of the danger zone. Now for their parents.

"Is that a side effect of the healing? The sleeping?" I asked Levi to double-check.

"Yes. They'll need lots of rest to recover their energy." He turned his head to stare into the distance moments before headlights lit the road.

Cricket parked behind me and got out. She turned to dig towels and pillows out. I beckoned her toward me.

Maverick's disbelieving glare landed on me. "You called her here when it's dangerous out?"

"Stop it," she snapped. "I don't want to sit at home when the clan's in trouble any more than you."

I tossed towels to Maverick and Memphis. "Pressure with the healing." I handed some to Levi. "Give these to Briony."

I tucked the pillows under Emily's legs, hoping gravity would have mercy on us and her diminishing blood supply.

Memphis and Maverick took breaks between healing sessions. Briony and Levi monitored the driver, giving me regular updates. I stayed by the car when I wasn't checking on the parents and hoped that my mate wouldn't be my fifth patient of the night.

～

I'D NEVER BEEN SO tired. Holding my head up took more effort than doing neck lifts with a ton of bricks. Emily Ohana was a quiet female. Loved being a mom and doted on her gruff plumber mate. I wasn't going to let her pass without a goddamn fight.

But worry the fight would take us both out took over. Logically, I knew I shouldn't sacrifice myself for her, especially without a guarantee she would survive. I was supposed to be more important, but that was all bullshit. Rank and status didn't matter, and others could lead this clan.

Didn't mean I wanted to die. I didn't want to fade away in front of the mate I was falling hard for.

This whole night must be a mix of morbid absurdity to him. A bunch of naked people trying to save crash victims. A mix of hilarity and gruesome. Yet he oversaw the whole rescue with a calm command. He was scared. The acrid tint mixed with his normal scent. He was tired and wired. So were my brothers and their mates.

Cricket murmured in Emily's ear, and if I had the energy, I'd hug the shit out of her. My twin's mate proved herself more the longer she was here. Emily was pounding on death's door, but hearing her kids were okay and needed her had located some energy reserves. Our bouts of healing were making more and more progress until Vaughn's hand on my shoulder gently pulled me away.

"Her pulse is steady, and her breathing is improving. She just needs rest now." He gathered me into his arms. "And so do you."

"Vaughn, you don't need to carry me."

He deposited me in the passenger seat of Cricket's car. Maverick and Levi were helping get Emily's mate Fitz into the back seat of Maverick's car. Maverick hopped in next to him.

"What about Fitz?"

"He's finally starting to heal himself." Briony came up beside us. "Levi and I will shift and head back to town. The rest of you figure out seating."

There weren't enough seats for everyone. Emily would go in the back with her son when she was recovered, and no one was moving the girl from the front seat.

"I'll fly back."

For a human, Vaughn had a good growl. "Sit on my lap while I drive."

I didn't have the energy to fight him.

The ride was cozy. Emily remained passed out, but her scent was stronger, her vitals clearer to my senses. I directed Vaughn to the family's house. By the time he and Cricket carried the kids inside and laid them on the living room floor, Levi and Briony appeared and helped get the parents into the house. Once the whole family was covered in blankets with water left for them, we locked up.

Vaughn wrapped a blanket from the trunk around my shoulders. "We need to go home."

"I have to talk to the council about the wolves—"

"Will they be back to cause more trouble tonight?"

The wolf shifters had had to run for hours while Maverick and I hunted for them. I wasn't sure if the crash was an accident, planned, or a seized opportunity.

I hated the certainty inside me that there'd be more issues.

Vaughn led me back to the car. Gordy stepped outside the house next door, his plaid flannel hanging open over ratty jeans and bare feet. They were neighbors. I suppressed my frown. Coincidence? Peridot Falls was a small town. Did Gordy or Edith know the Ohanas would be driving tonight?

"Everything okay?" Gordy asked, a touch of arrogance in his tone.

Vaughn stiffened, half blocking me from Gordy's view. He would need a while to get used to the nudity.

"Yes," I said casually, despite being wrapped in a blanket with my mate's arm around me. "You?"

Gordy recoiled slightly, like he wasn't expecting me to act like we were out for a walk.

The others were waiting on the doorstep as if they sensed the weak thread of tension. The show of support should keep the Ohanas safe for as long as needed. All of us carrying the family into the house would send ripples of introspection through the town, and I needed to meet with the council to discuss the wolves.

"I'm good," he said. His gaze landed on Vaughn and hardened. "Gotta be careful out there." Turning on his heel, he walked back in.

"What was that about?" Vaughn asked under his breath.

"Josh's father."

"Right next door to these guys?"

It was as suspicious as I'd feared. "I need to meet with the council immediately."

"Memphis—"

"Drop me off at city hall and run and get me some clothes." I wasn't asking. This was too important, and he couldn't fight me on it.

He let out a sigh. "All right."

I got into the passenger seat of the car, still warm from the child's slumbering body. My clothing was in my pickup by the Smalls' place. I'd worry about that later, just like we'd worry about getting the vehicles all cleaned out later—and ourselves.

City hall was dark. I got out, cinching the blanket around me. Before I shut the door, I leaned in. "Be careful. Just in case the house is being watched."

His brows drew together, but he nodded.

"You did good tonight."

"I need to get more supplies. Now that I've seen..." He shook his head and the muscles in the corners of his jaw clenched. "I have a better idea of what'll be useful."

"You saved them. We couldn't have done it without you."

He draped an arm across the steering wheel and leaned over the console. His pale-green polo was stained with blood, and his slacks were both bloody and dirty. "What you did was fucking amazing, Memphis. You can heal people. Do you know how amazing that is?"

"I'd rather heal than kill." I couldn't bring myself to give him a reassuring smile. "And I'm going to have to hunt a lot of shifters after tonight."

The struggle to accept that aspect of the job flitted through his gaze, but he held eye contact. "You do what you gotta do—and keep me updated."

"Thank you, Vaughn," I said quietly. I couldn't have done this without him. I couldn't have faced the deaths of that family. One of them would've rocked the community, but without Vaughn, even with me and Maverick, we might've lost them all.

"It's what I do," he said, and for the first time, I got a

sense of why losing his position in Las Vegas had been an adjustment he almost couldn't make. And I had an inclination of how momentous his acceptance of his position here, and of me, was. I'd never let myself forget.

THIRTEEN

aughn

I HELD Memphis in my arms as we soaked in our tub. I stroked the damp, satiny skin on her arms. The water was cooling, but neither of us was in a hurry to move. We'd showered off the blood and dirt. When I brought her clothing to city hall, Levi and Briony had brought over sandwiches and juice from the bakery. I insisted both she and Maverick eat while they were meeting with the council.

"We need a bigger tub," I said.

She chuckled. Her arms were draped over my bent knees. "We do. We'd need a bigger bathroom too."

"We could turn the office into a bathroom and make this the office."

"Is that how plumbing works?" A grin was in her voice.

"Not my area."

"Maybe we should…look at a new place?"

I stopped tracing circles on her skin. "You want to move?"

"I don't know. This is my house, but I'd like to grow into a home with you."

Grow into. I liked the sound of that. "Do you need more juice?"

"No, Vaughn," she murmured in a sleepy voice. "I just need rest."

"Let's get to bed." I picked her up with me. Water sluiced down our bodies.

She put her feet on the floor. "You don't have to carry me."

"You're lucky I let you walk out of city hall." Only the council's presence kept me from doing so. Perceived strength went a long way, and if I'd swooped in and picked her up, they'd have thought she might be too weak to walk.

She grabbed a towel and turned on me to dab it across my chest.

My dick twitched to life. I'd been talking it down for the last hour we'd been soaking. "Kitty, you need to get to bed."

She wiped down my body and curled the towel over my growing dick. "I do, but you're naked, and I hate to let an opportunity pass." She stroked the towel over my cock.

I crowded her against the sink. "You were so damn impressive tonight." And I'd been so fucking worried she'd tank herself. Burying myself inside her was another way to reassure my brain she was fine. She was in front of me, and she was fine.

But my brain also reminded me that she'd do it again in a heartbeat.

"You were the impressive one," she said. "I meant it. This far into the woods, we don't get your kind of knowledge."

"You have it now. I'll use everything I can to keep you from endangering yourself."

Her smile was understanding. "Hazard of the trade."

"I hate it." I took the towel from her grip and dropped it on the floor.

Catching a water droplet sliding down her chest, I continued to lick along the path it would've gone. I could drape her legs over my shoulders and put my face between her thighs, but she was tired. She needed the connection as much as me, but I'd keep it brief.

Straightening, I caught her mouth and lifted one of her legs. She wedged herself on the counter, giving me better access. One dip of my hips and I was inside heaven.

"Memphis, I need you to come for me." I needed to hear her cry my name. I needed to feel her channel convulse around my erection. I needed to spill everything I had inside her.

Tonight had been invigorating and terrifying and changed my view of these people. Instead of being low-key terrified of the residents of Peridot Falls, I had become protective in an instant.

I was the mate of their ruler. I was only human, but dammit, I brought something to the table.

Tonight, it would be a quick orgasm so I could tuck her next to me and feel her drift off to sleep.

Her body tightened. She was close. I didn't bother with her clit. Her adrenaline was fading but still elevated.

She was ready to explode in the next three strokes. So I made them good ones.

"Vaughn," she moaned.

"That's it, kitty. Let it go."

She hugged her arms around me like she needed more. I caught her mouth and plundered the depths with my tongue. I mimicked the thrust of my hips. She whined as she shook through her climax.

I let myself hit my peak. The release that had built with hers like it was answering her moans and cries with my own jetted into her milking body. I had my arms cinched around her so tight I could barely move, but I didn't need more than small jerks of my hips to finish emptying inside her.

Before I had a chance to sag and come down from my climax with her, I lifted her other leg around my waist.

She released my mouth and rested her head against my shoulder. The tickle of her eyelashes from slow blinks was on my skin. By the time I got to the bedroom and crawled with her under the covers, she was almost asleep.

Safe in my arms. Like it was supposed to be.

I was starting to understand the magnitude of my new job as her mate. Wolf shifters targeting residents. Possible treason from within. A dangerous dragon shifter? As I drifted off to sleep, I couldn't fight the anxiety that my medical knowledge might not be enough.

～

MEMPHIS

. . .

I FLEW low over the treetops. Tonight was perfect for flying. The moon was out, but the sky was partially covered with clouds, giving us concealment but also threads of light to aid in the search.

This time I was out with Levi. We were canvassing around the Smalls' farmstead. They'd lost a cow the night of the accident, but I saw it for what it'd been. A distraction. A way to draw at least me out of town so they could crash a car.

Fuckers. I'd rip apart every last one.

As well as Vaughn had done, I still worried about his reaction to the crash and the retaliatory shifters. He marveled over my healing abilities. He had ordered supplies and refused a trip to Minneapolis for work, citing a family emergency that kept him close to home. But there were times he'd go quiet. The worry he thought he was hiding from me would linger on his peppery-amber scent.

I didn't have time to sit with him and talk. He had his work, and I had to hunt wolf shifters.

I had called the pack the feral had been from. The leader had given me names and bowed out of the trouble. That was how it was with packs. They didn't want to mess with dragon shifters, so those who did were on their own.

The pack leader had three shifters that had been reported gone the night of the crash. She'd only noticed because she'd seen them speeding out of their little town north of Peridot Falls, and they hadn't returned.

I didn't ask her if they could be working with a dragon shifter in my clan. I didn't want speculation, and I didn't want the information out there. Gordy probably didn't think I'd connected the dots.

But I fucking had.

The thought enraged me. Gordy had a son, and if he —was Edith involved?—was planning a coup, then the kid could get caught in the cross fire. The council had already issued the termination order for any dragon shifter helping the wolf shifters and for the three wolf shifters.

Levi soared up through a break in the trees. He'd been searching in the other direction. I circled to the left and he dipped. Our way of saying we would widen the net, taking the same directions we'd had before.

We continued widening our radius for another hour. When I was close to calling it for the night, I swayed side to side to let Levi know I wanted to land. Touching down by my car, I found my pile of clothing and dressed.

Levi finished dressing at the same time I did. "Think they're lying low for a few days?"

"I think they're watching what we're doing."

"I'd love to interrogate Gordy."

My brothers thought he was guilty, but I couldn't do anything until I proved it. The council didn't like the idea of tapping his home, but I wanted to get this over with. I didn't need wolf shifters hunting my clan, and I didn't need a traitorous dragon hiding among my people.

I had a few missed messages from Maverick. He'd checked on Fitz and Emily. They had recovered but were still tired. Emily had gushed about being saved, and she wanted to thank me and Vaughn in person, but Maverick told them to stop by the next day, or even better, the day after when they were fully rested.

"I'd love to interrogate both him and Edith." I got

behind the wheel, and Levi hopped in on the other side.

The drive to town was quiet. I dropped Levi off at home.

He didn't get out right away. "Talk around town is very pro-Vaughn."

Gossip about my mate hadn't been anti-Vaughn, probably because no one knew what to think. No one expected him to stay, much less fight for me or the rest of the town. Healing a family would go a long way since Edith and Josh hadn't admitted to asking him for help.

"Vaughn is getting pro-clan," I said.

"And he's getting pro-you."

Was I blushing? "Yes. He is."

"Good to hear. When you saved his ass, I wasn't sure...he could handle you. Guys like him like to be in charge."

"Sometimes girls like me want someone else to take charge once in a while."

"I hope we're not talking about anything sexual. I'll vomit, Memphis. I wanted you and Maverick to open up more and let me in, but I have my limits." He shuddered.

I rolled my eyes, chuckling. "Get inside to your mate, jackass."

"I'm gonna go take charge." He rolled out of the pickup and jogged to his house.

The drive home was quick. I kept my attention on the shadows, but nothing set off alarm bells. I parked in the garage and went inside. Vaughn was waiting at the table with a plate of food.

"You didn't have to. It's late."

"Thought you might be hungry." He met me in the kitchen and curled a piece of hair behind my ear. I hadn't trimmed it since we met and had decided to grow it out. I liked his hands running through my strands. I liked giving him something to hang on to when I was sucking his dick.

I could take him right to bed and work off some frustration about being at a standstill for the last two days, but my stomach picked that moment to rumble.

"Come on." Vaughn steered me toward the table. "I used to make this chicken recipe for Cricket. It's oven-fried chicken, although you don't have to worry about cholesterol."

Sitting down, I dug in. The food was the perfect temperature to shovel it in. Shifting into my dragon always fueled an appetite, and today was no different. When my plate was almost empty, he went into the kitchen and dished up another.

"I already ate," he said, sliding the food in front of me. "I wasn't sure how long you'd be."

"Sorry to keep you up."

He had work in the morning, but he brushed it off. "Going to the office tired is different than being groggy by a hospital bed."

After I'd gobbled up every last morsel, I sat back with a sigh and enjoyed a moment of contentment. I didn't have answers, but I had a caring mate and a full belly, and those two things went a long way.

"I take it you didn't find anything?"

I shook my head. "It can be difficult to find shifter wolves from the air when they suspect we're looking for them, and maybe they're lurking on another side of town."

"You'll get them. What did their pack say?"

"Not a damn thing. Tossed the feral's family under the bus and said I could take care of them."

"What a cop-out. Can't you make them police themselves a little better?"

"We're fighting our nature with that. No other shifter wants to cross dragons, so..." I lift a shoulder. "It is what it is." I pushed a hand through my hair and winced. My strands were tangled, and a light smell of sweat clung to my skin. Vaughn's nose wasn't as sensitive as mine, but I didn't want to crawl into bed next to him like this. "I'm going to shower. Then I'm going to take advantage of you."

His smile was promising. "I'm all yours."

I ran through the shower and hooked a towel around me when I was done. In the bedroom, Vaughn had just taken his shirt off. My lips twitched at the way he'd neatly laid out his outfit for tomorrow on the dresser.

"You washed the dishes while I was cleaning up, didn't you?"

He glanced up, surprised. "Why wouldn't I?"

The perks of a fastidious mate. I wasn't a slob. My house wasn't a mess, but it was easy to take care of one person. Didn't mean I was losing sleep over dirty dishes. I woke and rolled out of bed to wear the first things I yanked out of the drawer.

"Nothing. I kind of like your attention to detail." I was about to unhook my towel when a muffled noise caught my attention.

Frowning, I glanced around the room. Were some of my clan out for a late-night walk or flight? While the temperature was hovering close to freezing? The cold didn't bother us for long, but we preferred to be warm and cozy in our homes.

"What's wrong?" He dropped his voice so only I could hear.

I cocked my head and sniffed. There was a scent blooming that wasn't right. It wasn't a smell I should have detected in the house.

"Is that gasoline?" My friends, the ruler of Garnet River and her mate, had been attacked in a building. Someone had tried to burn them out.

"I can't smell— Shit. I'm calling Maverick."

I wanted to tell him it was nothing. I wanted to say everything was fine. But the smell of gas was growing stronger.

I shut the light off. Getting Vaughn to safety was my priority. "Get down. We have to get out." A light bloomed outside the bedroom window. They'd started a fire. "*Shit.* Follow me."

I was towing him down the hallway, trying to decide which exit would be the best. Were they lighting a fire by each window and door?

A glow shone from the living room. There was a fire outside the front door of the house.

We reached the end of the hallway. The house was eerily quiet, but shouts could be heard from outside. I was about to lead Vaughn to the garage, where I could shift in the tight confines next to the pickup and plow through the garage door, when the glass in my front window shattered.

Bodies leaped through the wreckage, and a blast of heat hit me. I shoved Vaughn into the bathroom. There wasn't enough room to change into a dragon in the hallway. I couldn't retreat to the bedroom where they were likely trying to trap us or smoke us like a ham, so I rushed them.

A battle cry ripped from my lips, and I met the gaping jaws of one of the big wolf shifters with a solid punch. His head flew sideways, a yelp escaping. There was a second shifter behind him. I kicked the first one in the side, and then tight quarters and furniture be damned. I shifted, the towel hanging off me falling to the floor.

They were on me before the change was complete. Claws punctured my skin and the sensitive webbing of my wings. Agony flared through my body. I spun and lashed out, completing my shift. At least one body hit the wall.

Smoke was filling the room, and the blare of the smoke alarm was going off, blocking two of my senses. Blinking the sting out of my eyes, I tried to locate my attackers.

A dark form lunged for me, and I snapped my jaw. Fur and warm blood filled my mouth, and I held on, shaking my head and spinning just as claws scraped my side. The body banged off furniture I could barely see. The other shifter was trying to climb me and get to my head.

I clamped my jaws down harder. A drawn-out whine reached my ears. I slammed the body to the floor and stomped on it. Backing up for another go, I rammed into the couch or chair and tipped over. The wolf dislodged from my back, its claws gouging through my scales.

My dragon's belly was exposed from the fall, and the flames lit the room enough to see the lighter color of their fur. One of the shifters—the one from my back—rose, its teeth bared, and he went for my throat.

I rolled again but was too late. Teeth ground into my neck, and while my scales offered some protection, I was having trouble breathing, and the fire alarms were disorienting.

I swung my head but only smacked against the corner of the hallway wall.

The first wolf shifter I'd downed was struggling to get up. I flailed to get the second off my neck. Not wanting to bring the fire inside any faster than it was doing on its own, I had few other options. The two shifters were going to overpower me. They were more agile in this small space. My head was whacking off the ceiling, my furniture was a trip hazard, and I'd almost knocked myself out on the wall. I blew out a stream of fire. The first wolf screamed and dropped, smoldering from head to toe. The heat of my fire made the second wolf shifter drop, and I shot another jet toward him.

Now the wolves were lit up, the couch and chair were on fire, and Vaughn and I were in more danger than ever.

"Memphis!" Vaughn was in the hallway, a wet towel to his face, another hanging from his hand. "Can you shift back?"

I shook my head, trying to clear the confusion. I wanted to tell him to run, but if I opened my mouth, I might let out another stream of fire. I was borderline panicking. I wasn't scared for myself. Maybe a little.

"Shift back!"

His order calmed me. My scales offered some protection against the fire, but I was injured, and the flames were going to overpower us. I sank to my belly. I could wall off the fire. He'd make it. My skin was blistering and hot, and breathing was raw and growing more difficult.

He crowded closer. "Shift, kitty. Now."

My body responded automatically. My brain hadn't caught up, but weeks of being called kitty while he told me what to do and what he liked in bed was enough to turn me into my human form.

I was prone on the floor, coughing. Warm, sticky

blood was all over, and I didn't know how much was mine. "Go," I croaked.

He didn't. He slapped a wet towel over my face and picked me up. Then he skirted around the edge of the living room where flames were raging and ran to the garage, bumping my feet on the counters. He didn't bother to check before he kicked the door to the garage. Three times he nailed the panel with his foot before it groaned open.

The air in the garage was a little fresher, but the heat was stifling. The back wall of the garage was the same wall as the bedroom, and there was an orange glow outside the small square window. The shifters tried to trap us inside, and there was still one more out there.

I swung my head around. *No.* The garage door nearly glowed. It was catching fire and the garage would be entrenched soon.

I tried to push out of Vaughn's hold. Reluctantly, he set me down, and I dropped the towel from my face.

"Get the axe." I weakly pointed toward the bucket of yard tools I occasionally used.

He did as I asked.

I swallowed, my throat worse than sandpaper. "I'm going to shift and break the garage door down."

"Memphis!" The shout came from outside. Maverick. "Vaughn!"

I couldn't let my brother mess with the fire. "Stick to the wall," I told Vaughn. The fire inside hadn't spread this far.

I faced the smoldering door and shifted, weaving on my feet. The stretch of my limbs and my punctured skin intensified the pain streaming through my body. Attempting to escape was better than baking in my garage with my mate. I was crouched between the wall and the pickup, but I launched myself as hard as I could through the door.

Hot metal caught my wings, and I rushed out into a wall of fire. Whatever fuel the shifters had used, they piled it in front of the garage door, and I ran right into a burning pool. Agony blistered across my scales. My tender underbelly was the most exposed. The pain made me falter, stumbling to the side, but I disrupted the flames enough that Vaughn rushed out in my wake.

"Memphis, you're on fire." He yanked the towel tied around his face off and swatted at the flames with it.

I lurched away, tucked my ravaged wings in, nearly gagging at the pain, and rolled. Every moment was torture, but I refused to burn to death in front of my mate, my family, my town, and those murderous bastards. I flopped and flipped, trying to smother as much surface area as possible. My wings were shattered, the pain mingling with the rest.

"Stop, Memphis." Vaughn's panicked voice broke through my thrashing. "Stop. The fire's out. You're going to damage yourself."

His voice was muffled like he was speaking through a tube. I blinked, but my vision was blurry and my eyes just fucking hurt. I'd gotten a face full of flames and while my head hadn't been on fire—that I knew of—the scales were singed. Any soft tissue had fared worse.

I let out a breath. Who was wheezing?

Me. I couldn't bring myself to get up.

Vaughn was at my side. His scent was full of acrid smoke, but it comforted me. "Shift back, kitty, so we can help you."

Ugh, the energy to shift seemed monumental. So much work.

I blinked at the sky, and one eyelid got stuck open. Perhaps I was burned worse than I thought. Pain ricocheted through my body. I couldn't tell what was damaged and what was just plain ruined.

Vaughn hovered in my vision. A dark outline of the man I'd fallen in love with. Why didn't I tell him how I felt? I should've been brave enough to tell him.

I'd wanted to hear it first. A useless desire now that I was staring at a dark sky, surrounded by people and seeing nothing. I opened my mouth to speak the words, but coughing took over. More blinding pain.

"Memphis, please." He barked orders at whoever was around, gesturing with the axe still in his hand, yelling about wet towels. Something about a jump bag.

The *please* got to me. Fear clogged his voice. Terror for me. My calm doctor, who held his emotions so tight to his chest he could implode. A sigh leaked out, and I scraped together all the energy I could and shifted. Someone was screaming.

Me.

Senses were stronger as a dragon, but human skin was so damn fragile.

Vaughn hovered over me, nothing but a dark shadow. "Memphis, stay with me."

I missed seeing his features. The eyelid finally flapped closed. The other followed. And as much as I wanted to stay and hear Vaughn tell me what to do, I couldn't.

FOURTEEN

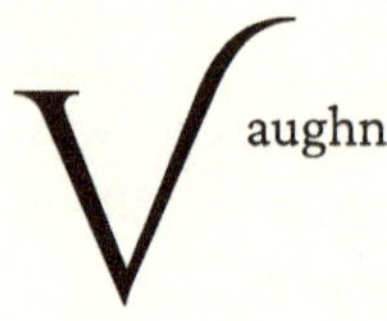

V aughn

I WORKED on Memphis with rudimentary field gear for an eternity. Maverick was at her head, infusing as much healing energy into her as he could, but he wasn't his sister. He could only do so much.

I'd take anything he had to offer.

Levi dropped to his knees next to us. "I found the bodies of two shifters in the house. They were in their human form, dead."

I was a doctor, but "Good" left my mouth.

"I got the third one when I arrived." How Maverick could speak through his tight jaw, I didn't know. Cricket was at his side, handing me whatever I demanded.

The third one. I hadn't even considered there could've been more danger after freeing ourselves from the gigantic pizza oven that used to be our house.

But Memphis's brothers had taken care of it. Now was my time to help, and I felt fucking useless. We were at a point where there was nothing I could do. Memphis had burns over most of her body. She looked like a boxer who'd done a million rounds with a furnace, and her arms and back were shredded from breaking through the garage door.

Levi put a hand on Maverick's shoulder. "Take it slow. We can't lose you." Maverick shot him a glare, but Levi remained undaunted. "She'll kill me if she survives and you don't."

Maverick scowled and eased up. I swept my gaze over my mate. My strong female had nearly been destroyed. The bastards were dead, but there was one more. Someone they were working with.

The pieces all clicked into place. Edith sitting on the sofa, looking around the house. Asking me questions like it was small talk. She was scoping out the place.

"That fucking traitor," I growled.

"We'll deal with him," Levi said grimly.

A fire engine pulled up to the curb. The volunteer fire-fighters were too late. They'd get nothing but practice putting out the flames in the rubble. I ripped my attention away from the group of dragon shifters rushing to aim their hoses toward the destruction. The planned destruction. They watched us. Knew when we'd gone to bed. Knew where her bedroom was.

A shadow circled over us, and I blinked up at it. A dragon.

"Fuck, it's him." Levi rose. "Stay with Memphis."

Gordy landed in the middle of the street. Neighbors had gathered on their lawns, huddled together to stay warm while gaping at the action. Gordy shifted to his nude form. He was big, not as tall as Maverick and Levi, but stockier. His nostrils flared. "I challenge our leader."

"You fucker," Levi said. "She's down."

I wanted to peel the haughty expression off the male's face.

"She's our leader. She should be strong enough to take on a few wolf shifters."

I rose, picking up the axe I'd abandoned next to Memphis while I worked on her. "Not when you spy on our house. Not when you attack our place after you light it on fire."

The corner of his mouth curled up. "Human." He said it like the one word should encompass all my failings, all his disgust, everything wrong with me.

Levi stalked past me, his fists clenched. "I'll fucking take you."

Gordy waggled an aggravating finger. "I challenged your leader. As long as she's alive, only she can face me."

"She's fucking—"

Maverick jumped up, hiding the way he swayed on his feet. All his energy was gone, funneling into his twin. "You can face me, you cocksucking coward."

The gotcha expression didn't leave Gordy's face. "You are not the leader." His contemptuous gaze landed on Memphis. "Get her up. I'm ready to fight."

"You're not ready for shit, you twat!" Levi shouted.

Rage ripped through the big man's gaze. I was foggy on the rules of challenges. I'd entered town while Memphis was dealing with one. Levi could fight Gordy— and he'd probably win, but it'd put the ruling family at a disadvantage. I couldn't remember the repercussions, but Memphis might lose her position. She'd be seen as weak. Too frail to run through fire after two wolf shifters in the confines of a small house. The family would be open to challenges. Our kids.

The small crew of shifter firefighters stood still like they were waiting to see where they had to move out of the way. Or worse—who'd they'd listen to if Gordy won the challenge.

I stalked in front of Levi. "What about her mate?"

Gordy's lip curled, and he scoffed. "What about you? You're useless."

Tightening my grip on the wooden axe handle, I made sure my voice resonated. "I'll accept the challenge on her behalf."

He guffawed.

"Fucking hell, Vaughn," Levi said behind me.

This challenge wasn't a disease I could retreat to my office and research before ordering tests. I was in the middle of the test. It was my life on the line. The future of my family. Unlike all my exams in med school, I hadn't prepared. I wasn't ready. But goddammit, I was determined.

"Don't do it," Maverick said. "Memphis can fight."

"I know she can, but I'd rather save her the *inconvenience*." My insult made Gordy's face purple.

Memphis would wake and take on Gordy. The obligation was in her blood. We'd rouse her, and she'd shift without hesitation. But saving her from further injury was only part of the reason I'd go through with this.

I needed to protect my family. *Me.* I couldn't hide behind my mate. I couldn't raise shifter kids and step back when they were in trouble. I needed to know if I could put myself in the path of danger that was superhuman.

"I get to use my axe," I said to Gordy, who hadn't

acquiesced. I wasn't an idiot. I wasn't taking on a dragon bare-handed.

He laughed. "Sure. Use your axe, human. And when I rip you apart, I'm still challenging our weak leader."

"Not if I tear your wings off and eat your head first," Maverick said.

Gordy shrugged. "Challenge accepted."

He was cocky. I would use it.

He shifted into his dragon—a few feet taller than me, covered in scales, with a tail that could smash all my ribs into pieces. I stalked back and forth like a caged lion. My breath puffed in front of me. I should be cold, wearing nothing but slacks that were halfway to ash, but red-hot anger-fueled adrenaline pumped through my veins.

Would it be enough to carry me through?

The logical part of my brain tried to push through. I didn't know a thing about fighting. I'd gone through school with my nose buried in a book. My weapons were science and a stethoscope, for fuck's sake.

I marched to the center of the road to meet the dragon, whose color was duller than my mate's. While he was larger than her in human form, his dragon was smaller. Her ruling bloodline had given her many physical advantages. Gordy didn't breathe fire, and he was arrogant.

That was it. My weapon could still be science. I gauged his reach and his movements. Shifter psychology wasn't much different than humans. Gordy was cocksure. He'd won the fight in his mind already, but it wouldn't take much to put him on guard.

I'd have to strike fast, unexpectedly, and be deadly.

I scratched my head like I was losing my nerve. I was quick on my feet and used to grueling work conditions and long days. I could use those skills. My punishing workouts in the gym before an epically long shift at the hospital before I moved to Peridot Falls would be one of my strengths. I didn't get out a lot, but I suspected Gordy didn't either.

I gripped the axe handle, cast a glance toward an anxious Levi and Maverick—and that was when Gordy made his move. The dragon lumbered toward me. I danced to the side, but his big head followed me. His eyes were as dull as his scales, lacking the bright-peridot contrast of Memphis and her brothers.

He lunged faster than I expected, but I ducked and rolled, holding the axe out to keep from impaling myself. He was too big to course correct and sailed over me. The end of his tail knocked into my head. I let out an oomph and recovered, flipping to my hands and knees.

I learned a little about his dexterity. The ringing in my ears was worth it.

Gordy let out a bellow. Levi bounced from foot to foot, like he was waiting for the word and he'd rush to my rescue.

I wouldn't need a fucking rescue. Memphis was waking behind them, her legs and hands twitching. When awareness hit, she'd be on Gordy, shredding him before he knew she was conscious. I couldn't let that happen. Her reputation was on the line, and in this town, that was as important as her safety.

Dancing to the side, I loosely held the axe in both hands. All the dragons I'd seen, including the Peridots, had lighter-colored bellies. It should be safe to assume the scales there were thinner, weaker, more vulnerable. Their arms didn't have a long reach, and they needed their hind legs and tail for balance on the ground.

Gordy lifted, his wings buffeting the air. He floated in the air and swirled in a lazy circle overhead, like he was showing off, telling me he had the advantage. But I couldn't fly, dumbass. Hovering above me like the world's largest mosquito would do him no good.

I could put on a show. I ducked like he could drop out of the sky like a stone and crush me. Physics didn't work like that. His wings and sleek aerodynamic body wouldn't allow it.

He looped around me, picking up speed. He was going to charge.

I gave my adrenaline some rein and spun. He needed to think I was terrified. I was scared, but I wasn't out of my mind petrified. Running down the pavement, I sent Levi and Maverick a hard look, silently telling them to stay where they were and, dammit, make sure Memphis didn't get up and intervene.

My shoulders wanted to hunch to my ears. Even in the dark, a large shadow loomed over me. Gordy was almost on me. I peeked over my shoulder. His determined face was aimed my way, his mouth hanging open. He might be smaller than Memphis, but I still didn't want his big teeth in my flesh.

Just as he swooped down on me, I ducked. He missed me with his teeth, and I immediately twisted, heaving the axe up like I was going to chop off a branch seven feet off the ground. The blade sank perfectly into the base of his neck. I knew not to aim for the sternum, or anywhere there'd be a high likelihood of bones.

The wooden handle jerked and nearly jumped out of my grip, but I held on and went for the ride. Getting dragged as Gordy face-planted into the road, I gritted my teeth. *Do not let go.* Road rash burned across my shoulders and back. I gritted my teeth against the fire. When we stopped skidding, Gordy was on his side. I dragged myself up using the handle. It ripped free, and I didn't wait until I had a good swing. I chopped at him. Dug the blade out and chopped again.

He jerked and flailed. I didn't get out of the way of his limbs. Claws raked my belly, but as long as I stayed standing, I'd block out the searing pain. Dancing away, I raised my weapon. Blood streamed over the metal and ran down the handle, making my grip slippery. Time to finish this. I skirted around his flailing. Hot blood stained the pavement, and his thrashing was spreading it around. He tried to roll to his feet, but I kicked his head.

"Stay down."

His roar was a strangled gurgle. He bunched like he was going to make a last-ditch attack. I struck, putting my weight behind the swing. The blade was buried in bone, but I put my foot on his neck and wrenched it free. He might not be able to recover from his injuries, but I had to make sure. I took another swing. Yanked my weapon loose. And again, until I severed his head.

My chest heaving, I staggered back. The relief passing through my mind didn't compare to the revulsion.

I'd killed someone.

I should feel worse. Maybe that'd come later. Maybe I'd still know then what I knew now—a menace was gone. People in this town could sleep safer with Gordy gone. His neighbors wouldn't have to worry about being targeted again.

Someone touched my arm, and I jumped. My hand tightened around the slippery axe, but when I looked into Memphis's concerned eyes, I dropped it entirely.

"It's a good thing you didn't promise to leave all the dragon issues to me," she said, her voice rough.

Gathering her in my arms, I didn't care what else was going on in the city limits. I didn't care our house was smoldering behind us. I only cared that she was healing.

"I could've taken him," she murmured into my neck.

"I know. I had to do it. For myself. For us."

"Why?" She pulled her head back to look at me, but I didn't loosen my hold.

"Because I love you, Memphis, and I needed to prove to myself I was strong enough to be with you and raise our kids."

"Vaughn." She held me harder, and we stood there, letting everyone else piss off for a little while. "I love you too."

MEMPHIS

TWO WEEKS HAD GONE by since the night of the attack. Vaughn and I were temporary residents of city hall. Maverick moved his office to the cabin rental building he and Cricket were setting up until Vaughn and I moved into a new place. Vaughn and I set up a rudimentary bedroom in the empty space. Our kitchen was now the break room. Between Vaughn, Levi, Maverick, and Fitz Ohana, the grateful plumber, we got the old locker room showers working, so we had a way to clean up.

My shower done, I was finishing up in the locker room. I shoved my damp hair off my forehead and peered into the cracked mirror. Our toiletry items were in freshly cleaned lockers. The council had tossed around ideas of what to do with this space, but now we knew. It would be a makeshift shelter for displaced residents. After Vaughn and I found a new place to live, we'd keep this space open and functional.

I mussed my hair. The top was long enough for a ponytail. The sides were a few inches long.

Did I look different? I inspected my rosy complexion. My eyes were the same bright green. I felt different but utterly the same.

I hooked a towel around me and made my way back to our makeshift bedroom. Everyone stayed away from city hall outside of office hours now that Vaughn and I were living here.

Vaughn was sprawled on the bed we were borrowing from Levi and Briony. He had plans spread out in front of him.

"Working in bed?" I asked and crawled in with him. It was the weekend, and the days since the attack had been busy ones.

We'd interrogated Edith. Not a fun job, nor had I been in the mood to be magnanimous. Vaughn had talked with Josh, and the boy admitted his father had broken his arm. Edith spilled everything once she learned Gordy had been killed. She'd vacillated between despair and relief.

I was so afraid to leave him.

He was a horrible mate and father.

I never regretted anything more than mating him.

Oh, god, what am I going to do? How am I going to survive without him?

After a thorough comb through her past, her belongings, and as much of Gordy's business as we could dig up, we determined she'd been abused by her mate. He'd hurt their boy and made her take him to Vaughn to spy on the house.

Communication between Gordy and the wolf shifters who'd attacked us had only been done with his phone and email. He'd gotten the bright idea after he heard they were unhappy with the termination of their feral family member.

Edith had moved her and Josh to live among the Opal clan. A new start for them.

Vaughn quit his job and was focusing on opening the business we'd discussed weeks ago. As for a home, between what he'd saved over his career and my gem hoard, we could easily build a nice place. Levi wanted us out by them. I liked the idea of being away from city limits. To have time off and space.

To let our kids have space.

Vaughn gathered his papers and set them on the loaned nightstand from Maverick and Cricket. "Thought I'd look at the plans while you were showering. I checked out big soaking tubs. I know just the one I want."

"I can't wait." I missed taking baths with him, even being crammed in the tiny tub of the old place.

We took showers together, and while I loved feeling him move inside me while warm water sprayed down on us, I wanted both.

He pulled me into his chest. "I'm working on the blueprints of the house tomorrow."

"You'll have to make sure there's a nursery."

"With a four bedroom, there should be no problem —" He pulled away to study my face. I couldn't hold back my smirk. "Are you trying to tell me something?"

I grinned, shyness taking over. "I took a test."

He propped himself on an elbow. "Just now?"

I nodded, biting my lower lip. "I feel like everything should be different, but it's not. My boobs are a little tender. That's about it."

His mouth was open, shock in his hazel eyes. A grin spread across his face, growing larger than I'd ever seen. "We're going to have a baby."

"We're going to have a baby," I echoed.

He pushed me onto my back and planted his mouth on mine. Pulling back, he gazed into my eyes. "Have I told you lately I love you?"

"Right before my shower."

"Have I shown you?"

"I think that's how this happened."

He chuckled and worked his way down my body with his mouth. "I still can't believe I thought my life was a nightmare." He was tender with my breasts, kneading them gently, placing kisses around the nipple before lightly sucking the pearled tips into his mouth.

I arched into him. I couldn't get enough of my mate, but I also couldn't hear enough of how happy he was, how much he loved me. I never thought we'd get here. "Vaughn."

"You need me to show you again, kitty?"

"Yes." No matter what, the answer was yes.

He brushed his hand down my belly, stopping at my clit. "Here?"

"Yes."

"Yes, what?" he murmured against the flesh of my breasts.

"Show me how much you love me." I was breathless by this point, rolling my hips into him, encouraging him to do something.

"I'm going to make you feel it." He prodded my legs

farther apart and inched down my abdomen. When he got to my belly, he paused and dropped a reverent kiss onto my skin. "You're so fucking perfect."

Seeing the way he looked at me and then at my stomach with the baby, who was smaller than a bean, filled my heart. Fuck everyone who thought I wasn't maternal.

He continued prowling down my body and licked right through my slit. "You're wet, kitty."

"Always for you." A groan ripped out of me when he flattened his tongue against my clit. He knew exactly what to do, and he wasn't taking his time. I exploded against his mouth and he kept going as tremors racked my body.

"Vaughn!"

"You're coming again, kitty."

And I did. Almost as fast as before. My knees were up to my chest, my heels on his shoulders. He gently moved my legs apart and rose until he covered me. Without pause, he entered me in one smooth thrust.

"I love how you fill me."

He was pumping lazy thrusts as he palmed my sensitive breast and thrummed my ultra-touchy nipples. I tightened down on him and he let out a guttural grunt.

"Fuck, the way you grip me." He kissed up the column of my throat. "And the way you come, holding nothing back. You're so ready for me, Memphis."

He wasn't all pet names in bed, but I stuffed my hands through his hair and lifted his head until he met my gaze. "You good?"

"Fucking fabulous." He slammed into me, hitting the spot that made me want to roll my eyes to the back of my head. "But I'm serious." His hazel eyes bored into mine. "I can't believe how lucky I got with you. I thought you destroyed my world, but you've given me everything I didn't know I wanted." He slid his hand between us to rest on my belly. "And everything I knew I did. You're my world, and I'll make sure you never forget it."

I didn't think I could come from words alone, but the orgasm washed over me, slow and sweet compared to the punch of his hips and the "fuuuuck" that left his mouth when he climaxed inside me.

He collapsed on top of me, and I hugged my arms around him. Rolling us to our side, he brushed the hair off my face. "You're going to be such a good mom."

Hearing him say that meant more to me than I would've thought. "You're going to be a great dad—and I'm not just saying that because you said I'd be a good mom."

He chuckled. "I meant spectacular mom." His gaze turned introspective. "I'm going to be there. Sleepless nights, playdates, school programs. It wouldn't have been like that in Vegas."

"It wouldn't have been like that anywhere because you were a workaholic."

"So were you."

True. We'd changed our ways. "So the nursery?"

He buried his face in my chest. "Mm?"

"Since you're a doctor, I assume you know it's possible we could have twins."

EPILOGUE

Memphis

I ROCKED in the outdoor rocking chair Vaughn bought to put on our back deck that faced into our spacious backyard that butts against the woods. He couldn't have found a more perfect spot. While I'd been working on helping the clan heal from the treason and brainstorming with Maverick and Levi to plan future builds and new businesses, Vaughn had purchased a plot of land and hired the builders. The contractors and construction workers had been mostly locals. For the jobs we couldn't hire from within Peridot clan, he'd contacted Garnet clan first, then branched out to other clans.

Ronan, the mate of Garnet clan's ruler, had come from Garnet River to help Vaughn with a lot. If I thought stern Dr. Vaughn was sexy, seeing him in a tool belt, a backward baseball hat, and a pencil shoved over an ear had derailed a lot of his progress as my pregnancy hormones and I had jumped him every chance we could.

The chair didn't creak as I rocked, watching Cricket rest a hand on her growing belly as she taught Maverick a game involving tossing bean bags in a hole. I had a garage full of lawn games. Who'd have thought?

I patted the back of Vega as she snoozed on my chest. The next ruler of Peridot Falls was a tiny peanut whose face turned red when she filled her diaper.

Vaughn opened the sliding door and stepped out, our son and Vega's twin propped against his shoulder. Vega and Milo were born shortly after the house was finished. They shared a nursery down the hall from Vaughn and me.

Things had been quiet since they'd been born, and I preferred it that way. Vaughn's acceptance of shifter life had infused the town with new mates. Human mates never failed to make me nervous, but having Vaughn and my brothers to back me up if things went south helped ease my mind.

Then there was the influx of other shifters. Peridot Falls was growing and, even better, thriving. We even had a couple of law enforcement officers.

Vaughn took the matching rocking chair next to mine. "Has Maverick let on that he could sink every bag?"

"I don't think he will for years. Cricket's been a little emotional with the pregnancy hormones."

He chuckled and settled into a rocking rhythm that matched mine. "That's to be expected."

"Briony told me she went to see you."

His smile was mysterious. "She tell you everything?"

Since Vaughn's new practice opened, he'd been busier than expected. He got to dabble in pediatrics. Kids still got hurt. He'd had to dust off his psychology training and brush up on more—both adults and kids needed to talk. Along the way, with my own pregnancy, he'd become an obstetrician. When he learned Peridot Falls had been sharing a midwife who lived in Garnet River, he'd taken over helping with baby deliveries. He was training a bear shifter who'd married one of the accountants in town and a wolf shifter from the coast who wanted to find woods to run and not be bothered. Both females were thrilled to put their nursing to use when they'd originally thought moving to Peridot Falls to mate dragon shifters meant hanging up the stethoscope.

"She said she's due after Christmas," I answered about Briony. "The Peridot family is exploding with kids."

"It's great, isn't it?" We shared a smile.

Levi came out of the house. "Memphis, you're getting sappy in your old age."

"Shut up. I like it."

He grinned and held his hand out for his mate. "Me too." He leaned against the railing to watch Maverick toss his beanbag wide. There was no way he was that bad.

Cricket planted her hands on her hips. "Maverick, you're going to sleep on the floor if you let me win one more time."

My twin's smile was unrepentant. He tossed another bag and it sailed through the hole without touching the sides. Cricket let out a disgusted sigh, but a smile played at her lips. She tossed a bag at her mate, and he rushed her. She squealed but waited for him to sweep her up in his arms.

Levi tightened his hold on his mate. "I could sink a few bags."

Briony dragged him into the yard. "Let's play."

Watching my siblings and their mates frolic on a cool fall night was priceless. When I glanced at Vaughn, I found him watching me.

"You look happy," he said.

"I am." I bit the inside of my lip. "Would you say I'm downright glowing?"

"Kitty, you're always—" His eyes widened. "Are you...again?"

I nodded. "It must be in the water."

He laughed, and Milo jerked at the sound. Vega squirmed, and I patted her behind.

"We're going to fill this house," he said. "And I couldn't be happier."

I'd forever be grateful for the day an overprotective brother drove into town to save his sister and ended up mated to me.

———

HAVE you read the other dragon shifters? It all starts with The Dragon's Oath.

FOR NEW RELEASE UPDATES, chapter sneak peeks, and exclusive quarterly short stories, sign up for Marie's newsletter and receive my first wolf shifter story FREE.

THANK YOU FOR READING. I'd love to know what you thought. Please consider leaving a review for The Drag-on's Affirmation at the retailer the book was purchased from.

ABOUT THE AUTHOR

Marie Johnston writes paranormal and contemporary romance and has collected several awards in both genres. Before she was a writer, she was a microbiologist. Depending on the situation, she can be oddly unconcerned about germs or weirdly phobic. She's also a licensed medical technician and has worked as a public health microbiologist and as a lab tech in hospital and clinic labs. Marie's been a volunteer EMT, a college instructor, a security guard, a phlebotomist, a hotel clerk, and a coffee pourer in a bingo hall. All fodder for a writer!! She has four kids, an old cat, and a puppy that's bigger than half her kids.

mariejohnstonwriter.com

Follow me:

ALSO BY MARIE JOHNSTON

www.ingramcontent.com/pod-product-compliance
Lightning Source LLC
Chambersburg PA
CBHW061446210726
48287CB00007B/2389